GIRL SCOUTS AT SINGING SANDS

"Come here quick! Tell me what you see."

Girl Scouts at Singing Sands (See page 82)

Girl Scouts at Singing Sands

BY

MILDRED A. WIRT

ILLUSTRATED
by MARGUERITE GEYER

CUPPLES AND LEON COMPANY
Publishers   *New York*

Copyright, 1955, by
CUPPLES AND LEON COMPANY

All Rights Reserved

GIRL SCOUTS AT SINGING SANDS

Printed in the United States of America

CONTENTS

Chapter   *Page*

1. Snug Down 5
2. The Locked Door 18
3. Hager's Hole 29
4. Night Sounds 36
5. Song of the Flute 44
6. The White Witch 52
7. The Treasure Box 61
8. Valuable Cargo 70
9. "Is Joe There?" 79
10. A Midnight Disturbance . . . 88
11. Spell of the Cave 96
12. The Private Road 103
13. The Missing Key 113
14. A Familiar Face 123
15. Judy's Mistake 132
16. Another Disturbance 141
17. Smoke in the Woods 150
18. An Urgent Call 159
19. The Hide-Out 168
20. Treachery 176
21. Trucker's Welcome 183
22. Descent into the Cave . . . 192
23. The Siphon 200
24. Help from Captain Hager . . . 207
25. Court of Honor 214

Chapter 1

SNUG DOWN

TWILIGHT was creeping up Singing Sands Mountain as the dusty station wagon turned in at the private road leading to Pine Cone Girl Scout Camp.

In the front seat beside the driver, Miss Louise Ward, troop leader, twisted sideways to smile at the six girls who rode directly behind. All were attired in the neat, green uniform of the organization, but each member of Beaver Patrol, it seemed, wore her dark green beret at a different angle.

"We'll soon be there now, girls," the troop leader remarked. "Pine Cone is lovely. We should have a grand vacation."

"I suppose it's too late for a swim this afternoon," remarked Judy Grant. She was one of the newest members of the patrol, a pleasant, dark-haired girl with saucy brown eyes and a ready wit.

"I'm afraid that by the time we're snug down in our tents, it will be supper time," the teacher replied, looking at her wrist watch. "Besides, we're all rather tired after driving from Fairfield."

"I'll be ready for chow whenever it comes," declared plump, good-natured Ardeth Padgett. "This invigorating pine air has given me a tremendous appetite."

"Given it to you?" teased Beverly Chester. "I'd say you always had it!"

The remark was made and accepted in fun. Nevertheless, Beverly had a quick tongue which occasionally annoyed even her best friends. At one time, the dark-haired eighth grader had been leader of the patrol. However, during the previous winter, an unfortunate skiing incident had caused her to become conscious of her personality handicap, and she had insisted upon turning the post over to Kathleen Atwell.

Kathleen was considered one of the most levelheaded girls in the organization. A natural leader, she always was thoughtful of others and had a way of getting things done with a minimum of fuss.

The other patrol members were Betty Bache, who wore her sandy hair in a short boyish bob, and Virginia Cunningham, an excellent athlete. Judy had nicknamed the three girls the "A-B-C's" because of their last names—Atwell—Bache—Cunningham.

All the girls lived in the little city of Fairfield, some distance from Singing Sands Mountain. Throughout the spring, they had worked very hard to save enough money for an outing at the official Girl Scout Camp on Morning Glory Lake. Now, as the station wagon turned into the private road, they felt that they were indeed at the threshold of a wonderful adventure.

"Our arrival here is somewhat different from the one last winter when we trudged into Maple Leaf Lodge," Virginia Cunningham commented, grinning at the recollection. "Remember?"

"Can one ever forget?" chuckled Judy. Contentedly, she drew a deep breath of the pine laden mountain air. "No one to meet us . . . a dreadful snow storm . . . the lodge closed . . . and that horrible caretaker!"

"A Scout camp is different, I promise you," Miss Ward assured the girls. "Everything is carefully planned. Nothing ever is left to chance. We should be there any minute now."

Eagerly, the girls leaned forward in their seats, striving for the first glimpse of the clear blue lake which they knew would soon be visible through the tall, stately pines. On either side of the curving road, they saw rustic signs pointing out interesting trails.

"There it is!" suddenly cried Betty Bache.

To the right, the girls caught a flash of blue water. A moment later, as the station wagon rounded another curve, they saw the camp itself, a cluster of tents, with main lodge and dining hall.

The station wagon pulled up at an office near the entrance gate. Everyone scrambled out, unkinking cramped legs. As the girls helped the driver unload dunnage, Miss Ward went inside to register the patrol. She was gone a long while. When finally she rejoined the group, it was evident by the expression of her face that something had gone wrong.

"Girls, I hate to tell you this—" she began apologetically.

"Don't say we aren't to stay!" exclaimed Beverly Chester. "That would be the last straw!"

"We're staying," the teacher replied, "However, there's been a mix-up on reservations. Another patrol, which wasn't expected until next week, arrived ahead of time."

"Then there's no place for us?" Kathleen asked.

"Miss Lubell, the camp director, is extremely upset about it. One tent, which sleeps four, is available. If we can make out with that for tonight, more satisfactory arrangements probably can be completed by tomorrow."

"There are seven of us," Beverly pointed out.

"The more the merrier!" declared Judy cheerfully. "I don't mind being crowded for a night or two. For that matter, it's warm enough to sleep out under the trees. We'll get along fine."

"Of course," added Kathleen heartily, "Scouts aren't softies."

"I knew you'd feel that way about it," Miss Ward said, pleased by the willingness of the girls to accept inconvenience. "Miss Lubell is taking me in with her, so that will make only six for the tent."

After registration had been completed, the girls were shown to their temporary quarters. They stowed their dunnage, spread their blankets and changed into informal camp clothes. Carefully reading the rules posted on a bulletin board, they learned that they would have only a half hour until the evening meal would be served.

"Let's see the beach at least," Virginia proposed. "We have a few minutes free time."

A walk led down a gentle slope to Morning Glory Lake, a deep bowl of deep blue, edged with a ruffle of green forest. The beach had been cleared of stones and sticks, extending for a long distance. There was a roped off area for safe swimming, as well as a dock to which were tied a sailboat and two rowboats.

Judy bent down to test the water with her finger. "Cold," she reported with a laugh. "It's just as well, I guess, because otherwise, I'd be tempted to leap in, clothes and all!"

The girls of Beaver Patrol met the waterfront director, their unit leader and several counselors. Members of other patrols and troops came by to chat and to provide scraps of information relative to camp routine.

Several of the Beaver Patrol girls were inspecting the outdoor ovens when the unit leader approached the group.

"I'm looking for Judy Grant," she said.

"Here I am," Judy said, separating herself from the other girls. She could not guess why she had been singled out for attention.

"I have a telegram for you. It came only a moment ago from the village."

"A telegram?" Judy repeated. She was startled,

and stood staring at the yellow envelope which the unit leader offered.

A half dozen fears assailed her. Her father or mother might have been taken unexpectedly ill! Perhaps her brother Ted had suffered an accident! At the very least, something must have gone wrong at home, and now it might be necessary for her to return to Fairfield before the vacation really started.

"Well, Judy, why don't you open it?" Virginia demanded. "Don't look so scared."

"This is the first telegram I ever received," Judy replied, a bit shakily.

Ripping open the envelope, she scanned the message. Her chubby face with its splattering of freckles became a study as she read.

"Bad news?" Betty Bache finally asked.

"No, not exactly. It's from Aunt Mattie."

"I don't recall having heard you speak of her," remarked Virginia.

"Aunt Mattie is a character. She's coming here for two weeks."

"To the Scout Camp?" Beverly inquired.

"Oh, no! Only to the resort area." Judy folded the telegram and placed it in the pocket of her slacks. "Aunt Mattie, as usual, must have acted on impulse. Anyway, she wants me to find her a nice cottage with reasonable rent."

"And you haven't a bed to call your own!" chuckled Kathleen. "From what I've heard, space is at a premium in this locality."

"That's right," agreed Ardeth. "I noted as we drove up the mountain, that there were no vacancies anywhere. Everything seemed to have been taken."

"I saw one place for rent," Virginia informed the group. "Remember that sign that said: 'To Calico Cave?'"

"Yes, I noticed it particularly," nodded Judy. "I was wondering if Calico Cave is only a name, or if the road leads to a real cave."

"A cottage that looked practically new stood on the opposite side of the road," Virginia went on. "It was rather cute, I thought. At any rate, a signboard in the yard said the place was for rent. A real estate man's name was given, but I didn't make note of it."

"That cottage may be just the ticket!" Judy declared. "I'll talk to Miss Ward, and if she says I may, I'll try to rent the place tomorrow."

Actually, it was nearly noon the next day before the girls gave further thought to Aunt Mattie's housing problem. Camp routine absorbed them completely. There were so many fascinating things to do, so many interesting places to explore, that they neither desired nor sought permission to leave Pine Cone.

A brisk swim in the lake preceded breakfast, and after the camp work was done, there were classes in nature lore and first aid.

At luncheon, however, Judy broached the problem that was on her mind, showing Miss Ward the telegram.

"I'm sure Aune Mattie wouldn't have made the request, if she had realized how difficult it is to obtain cottages here," she apologized.

"Why, I think it's nice your aunt is coming," Miss Ward replied. "Of course we'll help her find a place. *A Girl Scout's duty is to be useful and to help others.*"

"That's law three," Judy said with a relieved grin. "I just didn't want to put anyone to the trouble of having to take me to the village. Aunt Mattie's good fun, and I'll love having her near."

Later that afternoon the Scout leader arranged for all the girls in the Beaver Patrol to ride down the mountain to the little town of Milburn, a railroad and tourist center.

"I may as well tell you the bad news," Miss Ward remarked regretfully as the camp station wagon rolled smoothly around the curves. "You'll be crowded into a single tent for another night or two. Miss Lubell tried, but wasn't able to make other arrangements."

"Oh, it wasn't half bad last night," Kathleen returned. "We'll manage."

"Of course," added Judy cheerfully.

By this time, the station wagon approached a crossroad which bisected the main highway nearly at a right angle.

"There it is!" Ardeth cried, rolling down the car

SNUG DOWN

window. "The road to Calico Cave! That cottage Virginia noticed is on the other side of the highway, perched up on a slope among the trees. See it?"

"I do!" cried Judy. "Why, it's a darling little cottage! I'm sure Aunt Mattie would love it—if the rent isn't too high."

"All rents are sky high in this area," Beverly Chester warned. "I'll bet they're asking a small fortune for the place. Probably that's why it's vacant."

"Anyway, it will do no harm to inquire," Judy said. As the station wagon halted for a moment, she jotted down the name of the real estate agent, who offered the cottage for rent.

Twenty minutes later the girls were in Milburn, standing at the door of the Timothy F. Krumm Realty Co. office.

Mr. Krumm was busy making entries in a book, but he laid aside his pen as the Scouts approached his cluttered desk. He was a baldish, middle-aged man with a nervous habit of moistening his lips.

Judy introduced the group, and mentioned her interest in the cottage which was for rent. Timidly, she inquired the rental price.

"Let's not talk about price," Mr. Krumm said briskly. "First, I want you to see Calico Cottage. Five beautiful rooms, including kitchen, fully equipped, and a tiled bath with hot and cold running water. A collosal bargain! And you'll not find another cottage vacant within six miles of Morning Glory Lake."

Judy glanced uneasily at Miss Ward and remained silent. She very much feared that "the bargain" would be offered at a price too steep for Aunt Mattie's modest pocketbook.

"Well, I don't know," she began doubtfully. "My aunt isn't prepared to pay a very high rental—"

"Give that detail no thought," Mr. Krumm insisted. "I'll run you up there in my car. If you like the cottage—and you'll be crazy about it—we can come to terms."

Almost before she could think, Judy was escorted to the realtor's car which was parked at the curb. Miss Ward, Virginia and Ardeth also decided to accompany them, while the others elected to wait in the village.

During the swift ride up the mountain road, Mr. Krumm talked endlessly, extolling the virtues of the cottage he hoped to rent.

"It's a classy little place," he told the girls. "Brand spanking new! You'll not find a snappier cottage anywhere in the area."

"But the rental—Judy began again.

"Now don't try to get the cart before the horse," Mr. Krumm interrupted once more. "Just hold your ponies until you see the cottage."

Soon the car drew up amid the tall pines, in a lonely but lovely section of the forest. Mr. Krumm went ahead to remove the front door key from beneath an over-sized rubber "Welcome" mat on the porch. He unlocked the door.

"No neighbors hereabouts to bother one," he asserted, stepping aside so that the girls might enter. "You'll find everything in apple-pie order. Two airy bedrooms. Good mattresses. Nice draperies. Everything the very best—top hole!"

"It seems a bit musty," Miss Ward commented.

"Oh, the place needs an airing," Mr. Krumm replied, quickly raising the windows. "You know how it is after a cottage has been closed for a long while."

"A long while?" the teacher repeated. "Then you've had no recent renters?"

"That was a slip of tongue, a mere figure of speech," the real estate man said carelessly. "You like the place?"

"It is attractive," Judy said after completing a quick inspection of the kitchen. "My aunt though, will be alone. She requires only one bedroom. So I'm afraid the rent may be too high."

"Tell you what! I'll make you a special offer," Mr. Krumm said, eyeing the girl shrewdly. "That is, I will if you'll agree that the cottage will be occupied for the full period of the rental. Say, fifty dollars?"

"A week?"

"For the two weeks. You can't say that isn't a generous offer. Rents are high at Morning Glory Lake."

"It's a very reasonable rental, I'm sure," Judy agreed. "There isn't anything—wrong with the place?"

Mr. Krumm drew himself up haughtily. "What

an idea! I take a shine to you girls and offer you a real bargain. Then you think there's something wrong with the cottage! You think I'm pulling a fast one, handing you a cabbage!"

"I'm sorry," Judy apologized hastily. "My question wasn't tactful. The cottage is beautifully furnished. If Miss Ward says it is all right, I'll take it."

"Your aunt should be quite comfortable here," Miss Ward replied after a moment's hesitation.

"Fine!" Mr. Krumm approved. He whipped a receipt book from his pocket. "Now if you'll kindly pay in advance, we'll close the deal on the spot."

Judy had brought only twenty-five dollars with her, but Miss Ward advanced the remainder, knowing she would be repaid. Mr. Krumm then handed over the key. Judy asked him if he would mind if the cottage were put to use before the arrival of her aunt.

"The rent's paid, and the place is yours, for better or for worse," the realtor replied. "All I ask is that you don't come running to me with complaints, or a demand for a return of your money. The deal's final."

"That's understood," Judy agreed.

Having pocketed the fifty dollars, Mr. Krumm seemed eager to be away.

"You may want to look the place over more carefully," he said quickly. "I have a pressing engagement in town. Suppose I have your friends pick you up in the camp station wagon. Okay?"

SNUG DOWN 17

"Yes, that will be satisfactory," Miss Ward replied.

"Oh, by the way," Mr. Krumm said, apparently as an after-thought. "Better keep that door to the cellar locked."

"Door?" Judy repeated with misgiving. "I didn't notice a door. Is there a special reason—"

Mr. Krumm did not wait for her to complete the question. The girls were certain he heard and wished to avoid answering. At any rate, without offering further information, he tipped his hat and hastened down the weed-grown path to his car.

Chapter 2

THE LOCKED DOOR

MISS Ward and the Scouts watched Mr. Krumm drive away with mingled feelings. Already they were wondering if they had made a mistake in renting the cottage.

" 'For better or for worse,' " Juddy echoed the real estate man's words. " 'Final deal.' It all has an ominous sound."

"Especially that remark about the locked door," remarked Virginia. "But the rent seemed so attractive."

"Anyway, it was the only place available," Ardeth pointed out. "So why worry?"

Judy left the porch to inspect the foundation of the building. Stooping, she ran an exploratory hand across the crumbling motar between the bricks.

"This cottage may be brand spanking new," she remarked, "but the building foundation certainly isn't! Not that it matters, if the place is comfortable."

"I'd like to know what Mr. Krumm meant about keeping the cellar door locked," Virginia said. "Let's investigate."

However, before the girls could reenter the cot-

THE LOCKED DOOR

tage, a milk delivery truck rolled into the private drive. From the cab leaped a young driver with reddish hair and a carefree smile. A frisky black and white short-haired dog trotted at his heels as he came over to the porch with a wire rack filled with milk bottles.

"Good afternoon," he said politely, doffing his white cap. "I see you are moving in. Will you be needing any milk or cream?"

"I'll take a quart of milk," Miss Ward decided, selecting a bottle from the rack.

"How about regular delivery?"

"We've rented the cottage for my aunt, who won't be here for a day or two," Judy explained. "If you'll drop by later on, I'm certain she'll sign up."

"Cloverleaf supplies the best," the young man said. "My name, by the way, is Bart Ranieau."

"You must be of French decent," Miss Ward remarked.

"My father came from France, but I inherited my red hair and my temper from my mother. I'm a mixture—like Pete here."

The cheerful milkman indicated the little dog that was sniffing at Judy's heels.

"He's real cute," she declared, patting him. "You call him Pete?"

"He's mine only by adoption," Bart replied. "He kept following my truck, so finally I let him ride. Now he sticks like a burr. Never could find his owner."

Picking up the rack of bottles which he had set down on the porch, the young milkman turned to leave. Directing his remark at Judy, he said in an offhand way: "Your aunt is the hardy type, I hope. Not the kind that worries about strange noises?"

"We-ll," Judy replied, startled by the odd question. "Aunt Mattie is inclined to be nervous. Is there any reason why she should worry about this place?"

"Oh, the cottage is okay so far as I know," Bart answered evasively. "I'd be the last person to run it down, particularly when Old Krumm is so desperate for a renter."

"Desperate? Oh, dear, we thought it was just the opposite!"

"That you were getting a bargain?"

Judy nodded miserably. "Now it proves to be a lemon!"

"I didn't say that!" the milkman corrected her. "And the cottage *is* a bargain for anyone hardy enough to stay here."

"But what's wrong with the place?" Judy demanded.

"Maybe your aunt won't find anything out of the way," Bart said, edging off with his rack of bottles. "I shouldn't have said a word. Old Krumm would have a fit if he knew I'd so much as opened my kisser."

"Those noises—"

"Forget 'em. Forget I said a thing. You can take my word for it, there's nothing really harmful or dangerous about Calico Cottage."

The Scouts followed Bart and his dog down the walk, trying to learn more. But the young milkman obviously was in retreat. With a friendly wave of his hand, he sprang into the delivery wagon and with Pete at his side drove off.

"There *is* something wrong with this cottage!" Judy declared with firm conviction. "That young man spoke of strange noises."

"Maybe they have a connection with that locked door Mr. Krumm mentioned," Ardeth said. "Judy, I think you've rented a house with a mystery!"

"If that's all that's wrong with it, I'll be pleasantly surprised!" Judy responded, her voice grim, "I wish I could get my money back."

"No chance of that, I'm afraid," commented Miss Ward. Mr. Krumm warned us the deal was final. He may have taken advantage of us. That remains to be seen."

"Let's really inspect the cottage," Virginia proposed. "Mr. Krumm purposely took us through at a whirlwind pace, so we wouldn't notice too much."

Dejectedly, the girls trooped into the cottage. The living room was pleasant enough with a rug on the floor, a slightly musty-smelling davenport, chairs, a good reading light and attractive red calico curtains at the windows.

Bedrooms also were well furnished and ample

wardrobe space had been provided. Water ran rusty from the kitchen tap when Judy turned it on.

"Apparently, the cottage has been empty a long while," she remarked. "I guess Mr. Krumm tagged me for an easy mark all right!"

"If you were taken in, so was I," said Miss Ward. "All the same, I can't for the life of me see very much wrong with this place."

"Let's inspect the kitchen," Virginia urged. "Probably the drain won't work."

The sink proved to be an attractive new unit with shiny faucets and an unmarred enamel finish. Judy, testing the drain, found that it worked perfectly.

Ardeth had turned her attention to the big electric refrigerator. When she plugged in the cord, the machinery began to hum.

"Nothing out-of-order here," she reported.

Miss Ward meanwhile, quietly had been checking the kitchen doors. One opened onto a back porch and another into a storage room. The third one, which apparently led down to the cellar, was locked.

She turned the knob and rattled it a couple of times.

"Any key?" Judy inquired.

"None in the door."

"Why do you suppose it's kept locked?" Ardeth speculated. "Is there any reason why we shouldn't inspect the cellar? After all, it's part of the cottage."

"In a way, it isn't," Judy remarked. "I'm certain from examining the foundation of this place, that the cottage was built on an old base."

"I don't see anything so mysterious about a locked cellar door," Virginia asserted, losing interest. "Like enough, the basement is damp and musty. So Mr. Krumm advised keeping the door locked."

"Why should he tell us to keep it locked, when we have no key with which to open it?" Ardeth demanded. She was struck by an intriguing thought. "Say, maybe that key is here somewhere!"

"I know I'm not going to waste time searching for it," Judy declared. "I am a bit worried though, about that milkman's reference to strange noises. I wish I could be sure the cottage is all right before Aunt Mattie moves in."

"There is a way," Miss Ward returned. "We could sleep here for a night. In fact, it would relieve the congestion at Pine Cone Camp. We might try it tomorrow night."

"Why not?" cried Virginia enthusiastically. "It would be fun!"

"We could stock the cottage larder and have everything ready for your aunt when she comes, Judy," added Ardeth with equal zest for the proposal. "How about it?"

"I'd like to stay," declared Judy. "It will give us a chance to learn if anything is wrong with the cottage."

The girls remained on the premises another half

hour. By the time they were ready to return to Pine Cone Camp, their friends drove up in the station wagon.

"At least Mr. Krumm relayed our message," Ardeth said, as she climbed into the car. "Maybe he isn't such a bad egg after all."

From Calico Cottage, the station wagon followed a smooth pavement which wound in easy curves up the mountain. At a lookout point, the driver halted briefly to permit the girls to obtain a view of the distant peaks and valleys. They went on again, but presently were stopped by a forest ranger, whose green car was parked at the roadside.

"What have we done now?" Beverly Chester muttered uneasily.

The ranger greeted the campers courteously, dropping a handful of literature into Miss Ward's lap.

"Welcome to Singing Sands Mountain," he said. "This entire area is a national forest preserve. You're staying at Pine Cone Camp?"

"Yes, we arrived last night," Miss Ward replied.

"Girl Scouts always are careful about starting fires," the ranger continued. "I wish other visitors here were as cooperative. You're familiar with the regulations. The most important one is never to start a fire except in the designated places. You'll find them all marked on the forest map."

"We'll be careful," Miss Ward promised.

"My name is Arthur Wentz," the ranger ended

his little talk. "If I can be of service at any time, let me know."

Back at Pine Cone Camp a few minutes later, the girls found they had just enough time for a brisk swim in the lake before dinner.

Judy and Kathleen, who were good swimmers, were paired together. They tried their skill on the diving board, watched a group of other Scouts receiving instruction in Red Cross Life Saving, showered off and were ready for a hot meal when it was served promptly at 5:30 p.m.

Later, when all the girls had gathered for songs and a nature talk in the main lodge room, Miss Lubell mentioned a plan whereby all interested patrols would take part in a competitive first-aid expedition.

"It will work like this," she related. "Arrangements have been made for a forest patrol plane to drop messages to the various Scout groups which will scatter over the mountainside. The notes will provide fictional location of a plane crash. The patrols are to proceed as quickly as possible to the site of the crash, administer first aid and summon help. There will be an award for the patrol which accomplishes its mission first and with the most skill."

"If it's all to be imaginary, how will we give first aid?" Betty Bache asked in a puzzled tone.

"Everything will be worked out carefully," Miss Lubell replied, with a smile. "Although the crash is to be imaginary, counselors will be at the secret site selected. Notes pinned on their clothing, will provide clues as to the type of injury supposedly suffered. For example, one counselor may have an imaginary broken arm. The unit reaching the scene first, will be expected to care for the injuries exactly as if they were real."

"Say, that will give us first class experience," Kathleen declared enthusiastically. "I hope Beaver Patrol wins!"

Next day in camp the girls were given opportunity to brush up on previous first aid training, and patrol leaders received maps of the mountain area in the vicinity of Pine Cone Camp.

Throughout the day, when not otherwise absorbed by camp activities, the girls of Beaver Patrol pored over the map, thoroughly familiarizing themselves with every road and trail.

After lunch a telegram came for Judy from her Aunt Mattie Meadows, announcing that she would arrive in two days at Milburn.

"That doesn't give us too long to prepare the cottage and make certain that everything is satisfactory there," Judy remarked, as she showed Miss Ward the message. "Will we be permitted to stay at the cottage tonight?"

"I've talked it over with Miss Lubell," the Scout leader replied. "While she considers it irregular for any of the girls to remain away from the camp, she realizes that through no fault of hers or ours, one of the tents is badly overcrowded. So until that situ-

THE LOCKED DOOR 27

ation can be corrected, she is granting permission for three of the girls, and myself, to sleep at the cottage. We'll prepare our own breakfasts there, and then return here for the day's program."

"We're staying at Calico Cottage tonight then?"

"Yes, Kathleen, as patrol leader, will remain here with Beverly and Betty. Ardeth and Virginia will go with us to the cottage. The camp station wagon will take us to Milburn where we can buy necessary supplies. Then we'll be deposited at Calico Cottage, and be picked up again tomorrow morning."

The plan was acceptable to everyone, although Kathleen, Beverly and Betty secretly were a bit disappointed that they were not to be included in the party.

"Never mind!" Miss Ward assured them. "Perhaps tomorrow night, we can trade places."

At four o'clock, the station wagon came to take Miss Ward, Judy, Ardeth and Virginia to the Village. Most of their luggage was left behind, but each girl had packed a few essentials which would be needed for the over-night stay.

At Milburn, the Scouts sought a grocery store, there to make careful purchase of a list of supplies they had worked out. As she paid for the groceries, Judy remarked that they were to be used at Calico Cottage.

"Calico Cottage?" repeated the woman who had waited upon her. "Don't tell me you're staying at that place!"

"Yes, we are for a few days," Judy admitted. "I rented the cottage for my aunt. Until she comes, a few of the Scouts plan to use some of the bed space."

"You may like the cottage," the woman replied. "No one could hire me to stay there though!"

"Why not?" Judy inquired, instantly alert. "What *is* wrong with the cottage."

"That's what folks around here would like to know," the woman replied with an expressive shrug of her shoulders. "It's close to Hager's Hole for one thing."

"Hager's Hole?"

"Some call it Calico Cave." The clerk rang up the sale and packed the groceries into sacks for convenient carrying. She did not seem inclined to carry on the conversation.

"Please tell us what you know about the cottage," Judy requested earnestly.

"Really, I don't know a thing. I shouldn't have said a word. It's just that it seems sort of queer about the tenants."

"Did anything happen to them?"

"Oh, no," the woman answered. "But the last couple stayed only two days. They moved out in the middle of the night. Since then Mr. Krumm hasn't been able to find another renter."

Chapter 3

HAGER'S HOLE

THE sun had lowered behind the spruce trees as the camp station wagon unloaded three sober-faced Scouts and their leader at the doorstep of Calico Cottage.

"I'm not certain that we should stay here," Miss Ward remarked uneasily. "All this talk we've heard about the place makes me wonder if I'm acting wisely to allow the group to remain overnight."

"And I'm worried about Aunt Mattie coming here," Judy added. "I wish I never had taken the cottage. We've rented a lemon, that's certain."

The girls had been unable to glean any definite information from the woman in the grocery store. However, her observation that other tenants repeatedly had moved out, had filled them with misgiving.

At Miss Ward's suggestion, Judy had gone to Mr. Krumm to ask for a rent refund. He had rejected the request, impatiently assuring her that nothing was wrong with the cottage.

"I thought Girl Scouts had nerve," he lectured her. "What happens? You hear a few busybodies passing gossipy remarks, and immediately jump to false conclusions. When you rented the cottage I gave you a good price on it with the understanding that you'd stick by the deal. Now you come crying to me before you've spent even a night in the place."

"Girl Scouts do have nerve," Judy had replied, carefully controlling her temper. "We believe in being cautious though. And we don't like to be misled or cheated."

"It was your own proposition," Mr. Krumm retorted. "You wanted the cottage and you got it. I'm making no refund!"

So now, as the three Scouts stood on the porch waiting as Miss Ward unlocked the door, they were wondering what the night might bring forth.

There was little conversation as the girls quietly set to work making the cottage more liveable. Ardeth opened the windows to air out the rooms. Virginia made up the beds, while Judy and Miss Ward put away the groceries.

"You're not much worried about staying here tonight are you?" Judy asked the leader as she stacked eggs in the refrigerator.

"No. If I were, I'd take you girls back to Pine Cone Camp," Miss Ward replied. "Frankly though, I don't like the things we've heard. I can't imagine why tenants would leave here suddenly unless—"

"Calico Cottage may have a ghost," Judy supplied with a nervous giggle.

"Judy, we know there are no such things!"

HAGER'S HOLE

"Maybe by staying here we can disprove the rumors that have been circulating," Judy said soberly. "Now, if we could, that would be performing a real service for Mr. Krumm."

An inspection of the cottage and the grounds immediately surrounding it, proved reassuring. Save that a musty, damp odor lingered in the dwelling even after rooms had been thoroughly aired, the girls could detect nothing amiss.

"Our telephone is connected," Miss Ward reported. She had tested it by calling Miss Lubell at Pine Cone Camp. "It's reassuring to know that if anything should go wrong, we'll not be cut off from help."

"As we were last winter at Maple Leaf Lodge!" Judy added with a laugh. "Remember how that man who pretended to be a caretaker, cut the wires?"

"And the exciting time we had at Penguin Pass with Monstro the Snowman!" contributed Virginia, who had overheard the conversation. "Those were the days!"

"You speak as if our adventures are over," chuckled Ardeth. "I have a hunch we may have a few here at Calico Cottage before we're through."

The three girls became thoughtful as they reflected upon a recent skiing excursion to Maple Leaf Lodge on Candy Mountain. Judy, at the time, had been a Tenderfoot Scout. However, she had proven her courage and by passing difficult tests, had moved up in rank.

For that matter, not only Judy, but the entire patrol had won the admiration of villagers by the efficient manner in which the capture of a dangerous criminal had been accomplished. This story of the Girl Scouts' encounter with a clever impersonator has been told in the first volume of this series, entitled: "The Girl Scouts at Penguin Pass."

Judy and Ardeth peeled potatoes for the evening meal, set the table and prepared a simple salad.

"Anything more?" Judy then inquired.

"Not for awhile," Miss Ward replied. "The meat loaf will take at least thirty minutes more in the oven. Then we'll have dinner."

"Mind if Ardeth and I do a bit of exploring?"

"Not if you'll be back within half an hour."

"We will," Judy promised. "Want to come along, Virginia?"

"No, thanks, I'll stay to help Miss Ward with last minute things," she decided. "Besides, I had enough hiking this morning."

Letting themselves out the screen door, Judy and Ardeth walked through the aisle of tall trees to the main highway. Then, without any discussion, they turned into the narrow private road and struck off in the general direction of Calico Cave.

"No telling how far it may be," Judy presently remarked. "Or whether we can find it quickly. I simply have to see that place!"

"Caves always fascinate me," declared Ardeth, walking fast to keep up with her friend. "I hope this one has stalactites."

For a while the girls walked directly into the setting sun. The road was hemmed in on either side with stately evergreens which spiced the air with a pleasant fragrance. Presently, hearing a sound behind her, Judy looked back and was astonished to see a small dog following almost at her heels. She halted to coax him to her. He wagged his stub tail and licked her hand affectionately.

"Why, Ardeth, it's Pete!" she exclaimed.

"Not the milkman's dog?"

"It's the same dog, I'm sure. Do you suppose he jumped off the milk truck and is lost?"

"He doesn't act lost," Ardeth rejoined as the animal started on ahead of Judy. "In fact, he seems to know right where he's going."

"Maybe we should catch him," Judy said doubtfully. "He might get lost in the woods."

The two Scouts started after Pete, but the faster they hurried the more distance the dog put between them. Now and then, he would pause to look back and bark, as if to tell them that he thoroughly enjoyed the game.

Presently the weed-grown private road came to a dead end in a loop which would permit a car to turn around and retravel the route it had come. A weather-beaten signboard read, "To Calico Cave," its painted arrow pointing up a rocky trail.

"Come back here, Pete!" Judy called. "Why, you little scamp!"

Paying not the slightest heed, the dog trotted up the trail.

"He acts as if he's been here before," Ardeth observed. "Maybe he's trying to guide us to the cave!"

"We really should turn back," Judy said. "Oh, well, if we hurry, maybe we'll have time to take a quick peek at the cave."

Struggling up the sharp incline, the girls soon came to an opening amid the tall bushes. To their right was an expanse of limestone rock, badly eroded by the elements.

"There it is! The cave!" Judy cried as she discerned a small, dark opening.

Pete had gone directly to the entrance and stood there, barking and jerking his head, as if to beckon the girls.

"That dog has been here before all right!" Judy declared. "Otherwise he wouldn't be so excited about the place."

With Ardeth close behind, she picked her way across the rocky path to the projecting shelf. The cave opening was barely shoulder height and not more than four feet wide.

Curiously, Judy peered down into the dark interior. "It's just a narrow passage leading gradually into a deep endless hole," she reported. "I imagine though, that the cave may open up into a large chamber somewhere below. Want to explore?"

HAGER'S HOLE

"You and your jokes!"

Judy laughed and turned to leave. Ardeth however, crouched down to direct her gaze into the opening.

"I can hear water dripping," she reported. "Say, why do you suppose the name of this place was changed from Hager's Hole to Calico Cave? Or are they one and the same?"

"Ask Pete," Judy replied with a chuckle. "He seems to know more about the place than we do."

She whistled to attract the dog's attention, but he paid her no heed. Even after she and Ardeth started down the path, he kept sniffing at the cave entrance.

"Come on, Pete!" Judy called impatiently.

"Maybe he thinks he'll find a rabbit down in that hole," Ardeth remarked. "I hate to leave him here alone. I've heard of dogs losing themselves in caves."

"He'll come in a minute or two," Judy returned. "He's only trying to tease us."

Pete, however, did not follow the girls. At the bend of the path, they looked back again. Even as they called to him, he barked and vanished into the dark hole.

Chapter 4

NIGHT SOUNDS

"WHY, that crazy Pete!" Judy cried as she saw the dog disappear into the opening. "He went into the cave!"

Worried lest the pet lose himself in the dark cavern, the girls quickly ran back to the shelf of projecting rock.

Anxiously, Judy peered into the deep, rather terrifying hole.

"Pete!" she called. "Pete! Come back here!"

The little dog could not be seen, but the girls heard a muffled, answering bark. It seemed to come from far down in the bowels of the rock.

"He's a long distance in," Judy said anxiously. "What'll we do, Ardeth? Go after him?"

"No, we don't dare," the other decided. "It's dangerous to explore caves without taking precautions. Besides, Miss Ward is expecting us at the cottage."

"Pete may never find his way out. That's what worries me."

The dog's smothered bark gradually faded until no sound could be heard. Thrusting head and

NIGHT SOUNDS 37

shoulders into the hole, Judy tried again to catch a glimpse of the truant pet.

"Not a sign of him," she reported hopelessly. "All we can do is report to Bart Ranieau. He was such a nice little dog—"

"Do you see him?" Ardeth demanded as Judy broke off her remark.

For a long moment, Judy made no reply. Then she pulled her head out of the opening, staring at her friend rather wide-eyed.

"What's wrong?" Ardeth questioned. "Did you see a ghost?"

"You look down there in that hole," Judy urged. "Tell me what you see."

Ardeth moved in close beside her, peering into the darkness. A gust of wind ruffled her hair and nearly boled her headlong into the cave. She grasped a projection of limestone rock for support.

"See it?" Judy demanded.

"Pete, you mean?"

"No! No! Look far down the passageway, Ardeth."

Try as she would, Ardeth could see nothing save empty space. Now that her eyes were becoming more accustomed to the blackness, she could make out a white rock floor, and on the ceiling, a wet patch where grew a tight mat of lichens. But that was all.

"Look down," Judy directed again. "I'm sure

I didn't imagine that I saw something moving in the passageway."

Once more Ardeth directed her gaze below, and involuntarily stiffened.

"Now I see it!" she exclaimed. "Why, it looks like a moving light!"

"I thought so too," Judy agreed. "You don't suppose anyone could be down there?"

"At this late hour?"

"It doesn't seem likely, does it?"

"Maybe Calico Cave has a ghost," Ardeth declared with a nervous giggle. "Wouldn't that be something!"

Judy had peered into the cave again. "The light is moving away, descending along the passageway," she reported. "Ardeth, Pete may have started down there to investigate."

"If he did, he's welcome to the job! Just to look down into that inkwell gives me the jitters. Poor Pete! We'll never see him again, I'll bet."

"Someone will have to get him out," Judy insisted. "It would be too heartless to let him die in there. Miss Ward will know what to do."

Though she would not have admitted it, the moving light which seemed to have no explanation had somewhat unnerved her. With dusk coming on, she was eager to be away from the lonely locality.

"Since we can't save Pete without risking our safety, I guess we may as well hike for Calico Cot-

NIGHT SOUNDS 39

tage," Ardeth declared quickly.

"Okay," Judy agreed reluctantly.

Before getting up from the crouched position, she took a last look into the cave. The light had vanished completely and Pete likewise could not be seen.

The chill of evening was in the air as the two girls silently trudged back the way they had come. A rising breeze whipped the evergreens overhead, making ragged shadows and causing the needles to whisper mournfully. Far below, the White River remained visible in the dying sunlight, a wide, shining band of silvery blue.

At Calico Cottage, supper was nearly ready. Judy and Ardeth, however, had little appetite. Dejectedly, they related their discovery of the cave and their misfortune in losing Pete.

"You were wise not to try to venture into that hole," Miss Ward assured the two girls. "The dog may wander out by himself. Even if he is lost, the risk of trying to bring him out without a guide would be very great."

"You really think Pete will get out by himself?" Judy asked, brightening.

"He may. At any rate, he'll survive for many days. I'll telephone the young milkman and tell him his dog is lost. You're certain the pet was his?"

"It was Pete, all right," Ardeth answered. "He acted as if he'd been in that cave before too."

"Then there's an excellent chance he may find

his way out," the troop leader asserted. "I'll telephone the dog's owner now. Do you recall his name, Judy?"

"Bart Ranieau."

Miss Ward went directly to the telephone, but was unable to contact the young man. She learned that he roomed in the village, and was informed by his landlady that after coming in from his milk route, he had left without saying where he intended to go.

"If we can't get word to him by tomorrow morning, I'll notify the forest rangers," Miss Ward decided. "They'll know how to proceed."

As night came on, the girls washed all the dishes and tidied the kitchen. The very nearness of the cave and the knowledge that Pete was lost somewhere in its vast recesses, tended to depress them.

Virginia spoke somewhat wistfully of Pine Cone Camp, speculating upon whether or not the other Scouts might be having a ceremonial fire and singfest there.

"We're cut off from the fun here," Judy acknowledged. "It's my fault too. If Aunt Mattie hadn't sent that telegram, We'd all be in camp together."

"Considering the mix-up over reservations, the sleeping arrangement is much better here," Ardeth declared. "Besides, we don't want your aunt to have this cottage if it isn't suitable."

"It's a Girl Scout's duty to be useful and to

help others," added Virginia gravely. "At any rate, we like Calico Cottage."

"I can't see anything wrong with the place," Ardeth picked up the conversation. "Of course, it's isolated and a bit lonely off here in the pines. Now and then that musty odor hangs over the place, and one can't seem to localize it. The cottage isn't really damp."

"I've been annoyed by that odor myself," said Miss Ward. "It was especially strong when first we opened up the cottage. I wonder if it comes from the cellar?"

"With that door locked, we can't investigate," Judy responded. "What do you suppose became of the key? And why did Mr. Krumm advise us to keep the door locked? Those questions keep going around in my mind."

The evening passed slowly for the girls. Ardeth sewed and the others tried to read. As a chill crept over the cottage, Miss Ward lighted a heater which made the living room more cheerful. By eight-thirty, everyone was ready to go to bed.

"We must be abroad early in the morning," Miss Ward warned. "Breakfast at seven. The camp station wagon will pick us up between eight-thirty and nine o'clock."

Judy and Ardeth had elected to share one of the bedrooms, while Virginia and the teacher took the adjoining chamber. The mattresses were surprisingly comfortable.

Snuggling down into the covers, Judy closed her eyes, but was annoyed to discover that she was not sleepy. Ardeth, on the other hand, curled up like a kitten, and soon was breathing with deep regularity.

"What's the matter with me anyhow?" Judy asked herself. "I guess I can't take the comforts of home."

For awhile, she stared out the open window, watching the movement of the pine trees. A strong, cool breeze had arisen. It flapped the calico draperies and whistled around the corners of the flimsily-built cottage.

Judy resolutely tried not to think of Calico Cave or poor Pete, but the harder she struggled to banish the unpleasant recollection, the more clearly it emerged. She could visualize the little dog, wandering helplessly deeper and deeper into the cavern, always searching for an exit which never materialized.

"I'm becoming positively morbid!" she told herself sternly. "Enough of this!"

Judy tossed off the blankets and taking care not to disturb Ardeth, went quickly to the kitchen for a drink of water.

The cottage was very still. Now that she was abroad, Judy began to regret that she had left her comfortable, warm bed. The kitchen was icy cold and the only light came from a half moon which shone eerily through the windows.

NIGHT SOUNDS

Judy drank a glass of water in the darkness, preferring not to disturb any of the sleepers by switching on a light. In the kitchen, the damp, unpleasant odor which the girls had noted earlier, seemed especially strong.

"I'm sure it comes from the basement," she thought, sniffing the air close to the locked door. "Maybe this is why Mr. Krumm wants us to keep it closed. But what can cause such an odor?"

Judy had started to move away when she was startled by an unusal sound which seemed to come from beneath the floor of the kitchen. The noise assaulted her ears as a series of loud thumps.

"Gracious!" Judy thought, backing a step away from the locked cellar door. "What's going on down there in the basement? Maybe this place does have a ghost!"

If the loud thumping, bumping noise had startled Judy, she was to suffer an even greater shock.

As she held herself rigid, straining to catch the slightest sound, there arose from below, the clear melodious notes of a flute!

Chapter 5

SONG OF THE FLUTE

JUDY stood transfixed, listening tensely. The musical notes now had died out and in the kitchen there was only silence. Had the strange notes of the flute been no more than a trick of the imagination?

Suddenly she was aware of a sound in the room beyond the kitchen. Judy whirled to see a white apparition framed in the doorway. She uttered a choked cry and then laughed aloud in relief. The figure was no ghost, only Miss Ward in a white bathrobe.

"Did I startle you?" the teacher asked in a whisper. "Is it you, Judy?"

"Yes, I couldn't sleep. I came out here to get a drink of water. For a minute I thought you were a ghost from the basement!"

"Oh, Judy!" Miss Ward reproved. "What nonsense!"

"I was joking," Judy said hastily. "Of course, everyone knows there are no ghosts. All the same, that sound was unnerving."

"Sound? What sound, Judy?"

"Well, it seemed to come from the cellar. First,

I heard a series of loud thumps. Then, I thought I heard someone playing the flute."

"Perhaps the sound drifted in from outside the cottage."

"I'm sure it didn't, Miss Ward."

For several minutes the Scout leader listened attentively, but the noises which had disturbed Judy were not to be heard again.

"It is very late," she said finally. "Judy, you must go back to bed."

"I'm sorry to have awakened you. I tried to be quiet." As Judy started across the kitchen, the badly constructed floor creaked beneath her slippered feet. She had reached the living room doorway, when she was brought up short by the high pitched note of a musical instrument.

"There it is again, Miss Ward!" she whispered, grasping the teacher's arm. "A flute! Hear it?"

"Yes, I do," the Scout leader replied. "It certainly sounds like a reed or a wind instrument." She stood very still, listening.

From below the flooring issued a series of musical notes, tuneless but not displeasing to the ear. Then the kitchen again was enveloped in silence.

"It wasn't my imagination, Miss Ward. You heard it too!"

"No, you didn't imagine it, Judy," the teacher soberly agreed. "The sound came from the basement, or so it seemed to me."

Crossing to the cellar door, Miss Ward twisted

the knob and pulled hard on it. "It's still locked," she murmured. "I begin to understand why Mr. Krumm was unwilling to make a refund on the rent."

"This explains why the other tenants moved out so suddenly."

"It may," Miss Ward acknowledged. "Evidently, there is a very good reason for keeping this door locked."

"You don't suppose—anyone—could be down there?" Judy said falteringly. "Maybe locked in?"

"I'm afraid you've been watching too many television thrillers.'

"I guess so," Judy admitted, laughing shakily. "My theory is wild all right. How do you explain the flute?"

"I don't. However, I intend to talk to Mr. Krumm tomorrow. If this cottage has a mystery or any possible danger, it is his duty to inform us completely. Now get to bed, Judy. I'll sit up for awhile."

Next morning, when Judy awoke from a deep slumber, bright sunlight was streaming through the slats of the venetian blinds. Ardeth already was up and dressed.

"Breakfast in ten minutes," she informed Judy, giving her a hard shake. "If you don't get a move on, we'll not be ready by the time the camp station wagon calls for us."

"I guess I overslept," Judy mumbled, pulling out

of bed and groping blindly for her shirt and slacks. "Is everything all right?"

"Is everything all right?" Ardeth echoed, starting to air the bed. "What could go wrong so early in the morning?"

"I was just wondering, that's all," Judy answered, deciding to postpone the tale of the flute until after breakfast. "What smells so utterly delicious?"

"Bacon. Miss Ward and Virginia are cooking it. We've been assigned to the dishes."

Judy dressed speedily, helped Ardeth tidy the bedroom, and was ready in time to help carry dishes to the breakfast table.

Miss Ward herself broached the subject of the strange sounds which had been heard in the basement during the night.

"I don't wish to alarm anyone," she asserted, pouring hot chocolate. "I feel though, that if we are to stay here, we must be on the alert. Furthermore, I intend to ask Mr. Krumm for an explanation. I am sure there is one, and that he can provide it."

"If he will," Judy added. "He certainly wasn't passing out any information when he rented this cottage. I don't know what to do about Aunt Mattie."

"Fortunately, she won't be here for a day or two," Miss Ward replied. "We'll have a little time in which to try to clear up the situation."

"That Pete!" he remarked. "He's a natural-born spelunker."

"A what?" demanded Judy.

"A spelunker. That's what modern cave explorers call themselves. The science of cave exploring is called speleology."

Bart motioned for the girls to step over to the milk wagon. Peering in, they saw Pete sprawled comfortably on a rug, lying on the floor. He was fast asleep, his head resting on his forepaws.

"Pete found his own way out of the cave, as he usually does," Bart explained. "I've tried to keep him out, but no soap. One of these days, he may lose his life in there."

"Well, at any rate, he's safe now," Judy declared, greatly relieved. "Is the cave very deep?"

"The exit never has been found."

"Really?" Ardeth's eyes opened wide. "I guess Calico Cave is an unsafe place."

"One shouldn't venture in very far without a guide. Some ten years ago, a very courageous man whom I knew rather well, lost his life down there. He was seeking the cave exit. Since then, no one has ventured past the point where he was last seen."

Judy inquired if Calico Cave and Hager's Hole were one and the same place. Bart replied that they were identical.

"For years the cave was known as Hager's Hole," he explained. "It was named for old Captain Hager, who once owned this property."

"Our cottage?" Virginia asked in astonishment.

"Not the cottage. But the Hager home used to stand in the same location. Mr. Krumm bought the place not so long ago. He tore down the old house and put up a new cottage on the original foundation. Folks advised him not to do it, but no one can tell Krumm anything!"

"He's had a little trouble renting the cottage?" Judy probed.

"Oh, renters came along fast enough, but they wouldn't stay!" the milkman chuckled. "Some of 'em, it seems, were alergic to strange sounds. I take it you folks spent a comfortable night?"

"We were disturbed once," Miss Ward answered. "Nothing serious. We fancied we heard a flute player."

"No ghosts?" Bart asked, grinning.

"Nary a ghost," Miss Ward returned. "Naturally we were a bit disturbed about the music, and intend to seek an explanation."

"M. Ranieau, you seem to be quite familiar with Calico Cave," Judy remarked pointedly. "Could you, by chance, tell us why the name was changed, and maybe explain the mystery of the cottage?"

"Maybe I could," Bart said, grinning in an odd way. "I like you folks. You have more nerve than those other renters. Maybe, if you ask pretty, I'll tell you the story of the Old White Witch."

"It wasn't the old witch," Bart assured her. "She's a harmless old gal and has stayed fixed for a thousand years, more or less. I can't guess who might be down in the cave, because folks hereabouts seldom venture in."

"You spoke of former Calico Cottage renters moving out because of strange sounds which disturbed them," Miss Ward reminded the young milkman. "Can you tell us more about it?"

"Did the other folks ever hear a flute player?" interposed Ardeth.

"Seems to me I heard some such talk."

"And loud banging noises at night?" demanded Judy.

"I reckon so."

"Tell us everything!" urged Virginia. "Is Calico Cottage supposed to be haunted? Is that why Mr. Krumm has trouble keeping his renters?"

"All I know is what I hear," Bart replied evasively. "I wouldn't have told you about the White Witch, only I could tell that you Scouts aren't easily scared."

"Is there any connection between Calico Cottage and the Witch?" Judy questioned.

"Only as she's supposed to have cast her spell over the place. The last tenants had a cat. One night she became scared at some noise and leaped through a window, shattering the glass. The folks moved out, came dawn. I know because I met 'em as they were driving away. Tried to talk 'em into

"Bart didn't tell you *why* the man lost his life," Mr. Krumm said, without answering the inquiry. "No, he just filled you up with a lot of nonsense about a White Witch."

"She doesn't really cast a spell over the cottage?" Judy asked mischievously.

Mr. Krumm's normally florid face became even redder. He sucked in his breath, moistened his lips, and then launched into another vehement denial that anything was wrong with Calico Cottage.

"I'm sick of all this gossipy talk!" he ended his tirade. "I'm sick of losing tenants! I'm so weary of it, that I'm willing to pay good money to disprove all the contemptible stories."

The Scouts remained respectfully silent.

"Bart has convinced you, I suppose, that you should move out," Mr. Krumm went on. Without giving anyone an opportunity to deny the statement, he continued: "All right, suppose I admit that former tenants have complained about the cottage having strange noises at night? There must be an explanation for it—a logical, sensible one."

"We'll go along with you on that theory," Miss Ward replied. "You have a proposition, Mr. Krumm?"

"Yes, I have. It's all bunk about Calico Cave or the cottage having a ghost. If you'll stay here for two weeks, and disprove the story, I'll refund your rent payment. What d'you say?"

Ardeth, Virginia and Judy gazed questioningly at their leader, awaiting her decision.

"We would prefer a rent refund with no strings attached," the teacher suggested.

"Sorry, I can't do that. After all, I'm not in business for my health. This cottage has been an expensive proposition. What do you say?"

"We'll consider your offer," Miss Ward said quietly. "We'll remain for another night and make our decision after that. However, if we do make the test, it will not be for commerical reasons, but only to safeguard Judy's aunt."

Chapter 7

THE TREASURE BOX

PINE Cone Camp seemed strangely deserted when Miss Ward, Ardeth, Judy and Virginia arrived there at nine o'clock in the station wagon.

Seeking the tent which had been assigned to the Beaver Patrol unit, the new arrivals found it quite deserted.

"Where is everyone?" Ardeth asked in perplexity. "Surely not on a hike so early?"

Swimming suits hung on the clothes lines, attesting to the fact that the campers already had enjoyed an early morning plunge in Morning Glory Lake.

"Look!" Judy suddenly cried, pointing toward a cleared area some distance away at the edge of the forest. "Everyone is over there! Let's see what's doing."

Hurrying over to the group, the girls could not at first discern what it was that had drawn the interest of the entire camp.

Gradually, however, they edged deeper into the assembly and saw that the other Scouts were taking turns peering into a large wooden box, covered with a wire screen.

"What in the world?" Virginia speculated.

Just then Beverly, Kathleen and Betty caught sight of their patrol mates in the crowd, and joined them. Judy asked the cause of the excitement.

"Oh, you girls have missed all the fun, being stuck down there at Calico Cottage," Kathleen told her. "We've started a treasure box."

"What is that?"

"Look in it and youll see!"

The other Scouts moved aside to make way for Judy and the newcomers. Gazing into the box, they were amazed to see all manner of strange animals and insects.

"Its a nature treasure chest!" Kathleen informed her friends. "We already have a mouse, a spider, and three varieties of turtles. Each patrol is supposed to contribute an animal, bird or unusual insect."

"Does Beaver Patrol have an entry?" Judy asked.

"Not yet. Beverly very nearly caught a little chipmunk, but he eluded her. We're depending upon you girls to help us."

"We will," Ardeth promised. "Just give us time to get our thoughts adjusted, and we'll come up with a prize winner."

"There are to be no duplications," Kathleen warned. "All the patrols are working on it, so we'll have to get busy."

"How about a little garter snake?" suggested Ardeth thoughtfully.

THE TREASURE BOX 63

"If Beaver Patrol goes for that, you'll have to produce the snake," Kathleen replied with a shudder. "No snakes for me!"

"I vote we put Ardeth in charge of finding a patrol entry for the treasure box," proposed Betty Bache, who had joined the other girls. "She'll get a big boot out of the job."

"I'll be glad to take it over," Ardeth offered, for she thoroughly enjoyed the study of nature and had no fear of animals or insects.

"Good!" Kathleen approved. "That takes a load off my mind."

The blowing of a bugle, summoned all the campers to assembly. Miss Lubell waited until all the Scouts had gathered, and then signalled for silence. It was evident that she had a most important announcement.

"Girls," she began," we had planned a hike to Indian Falls this morning, but it will be necessary to make a change."

A chorus of groans met this announcement, for the girls had looked forward to the outing and outdoor cookery.

"However, we have other interesting plans," the director went on quickly. "The Civil Air Patrol has notified me that it can make a plane available for the first-aid and exploration excursion I mentioned earlier. But today is the only time the Service will be able to cooperate. Accordingly, we've decided to go ahead. All patrols desiring to compete, should sign up at once. Your counselors will provide full details."

The girls were informed that at ten o'clock all competing patrols would hike a quarter of a mile to Flat Top, an area relatively level and clear of trees.

According to the plan, a Civil Air Patrol plane would fly over the section to drop a message which would give Scouts notification of a fake plane crash. The general location of the accident likewise would be given. Starting with equal information, the units were expected to separate and compete in trying to be the first to reach the designated locality.

Once there, the Scouts were to give first aid treatment to the imaginary victims, and proceed exactly as if the accident were a real one. Three girls from the Garden City Patrol had volunteered to act as the injured passengers of the plane crash. Notes would be pinned to their clothing, stating the nature of their supposed injuries.

Kathleen, Judy, Betty and Beverly teamed up as one exploring unit, representing Beaver Patrol. Ardeth and Virginia decided not to enter the competition, preferring to remain behind to search for a suitable wild pet to add to the treasure box collection.

Shortly after ten o'clock, the representatives of seven patrols were encamped on the table top, anxiously scanning the sky for a glimpse of the expected plane. All the girls had dressed sensibly in heavy shirts, slacks and stout climbing boots. Faces and necks were protected from the sun, but even so, the rays bore fiercely down upon their backs as they sat impatiently waiting.

"Won't that plane ever come?" Beverly fretted, wiping perspiration from her neck. "We've been here an age now!"

"Only ten minutes," Kathleen corrected.

"Well, it seems a year. Maybe there's been a mix-up about plans," Beverly went on. "I wish I'd stayed in camp. This trip will be hard and tiring."

"Good experience though," Judy said, continuing to scan the azure, almost cloudless sky. "It will be a test of skill to find our way to the right place, administer first aid, make improvised litters and carry our victims to help."

"I hope we're the first to get there," Kathleen declared. "So far, Beaver Patrol hasn't shown up too well in the camp competitions. That's because all of the girls haven't been together, especially in the evening. This is our chance."

Judy suddenly sprang to her feet. She had been the first in the group to sight the Civil Air Patrol plane winging in from the east.

"Here it comes!" she cried. "They'll be dropping a message in a moment. Watch sharp!"

All of the patrols now were alert and ready. The Scouts who had equipped themselves with field glasses, trained them on the approaching plane.

Its wings flashing in the sunlight, the ship came

in low enough for the girls to see the forms of the pilot and his passenger. Three times the plane circled the tableland. Then on the fourth trip over, the message tube was dropped.

It missed the open table top by twenty feet, landing amid the trees and brush just below where the Beaver Patrol girls had taken their stand.

"Come on," Judy shouted, starting off at a run. "I saw where it dropped!"

There was a mad scramble to see who would be the first to reach the message tube. According to the rules of the competition, the directions, once read, could not be kept, but must be left behind for other patrols.

Plunging through the underbrush, Judy was the first to seize upon the shining metal tube. As she opened it to remove the message which had been folded within, Beverly, Kathleen and Betty crowded close to read the directions.

"Plane crash at 9:48 a.m. on Hermit's Ridge," Kathleen discerned the writing. "Three passengers in need of help."

"Hermit's Ridge!" Beverly explained. "Where is that?"

Judy already was consulting her map of the region.

"You might know its a difficult climb from here!" she exclaimed. "We have several choices of a route. We can take the short, hard climb—no trail.

That way, it looks to be approximately a mile and a half from here."

"What are the other choices?" Kathleen questioned.

"We can follow the main highway three quarters of the way, and then make a short climb on Lone Pine Trail. Our third choice is to descend from here to Rocky Point Path and keep on it all the way."

"I'm for taking the shortest route even if it will mean a harder climb," Beverly said at once." Let's go!"

"Hold on," Judy directed, continuing to study the map. "Im in favor of the road myself. It may be longer, but it's a lot faster, easier walking most of the way."

"Furthermore, we may be able to catch a ride part of the distance," Kathleen added. "That would be within the rules. The patrol wins that gets first to Hermit's Ridge and accomplishes its first aid mission."

"I'm in favor of the road too," Betty Bache asserted, siding with Kathleen and Judy. The various choice of routes is a test of judgment as well as endurance."

Leaving the message for the other patrols to read, the four girls quickly descended rugged terrain to the paved highway.

"I think we're making a mistake," Beverly insisted, shifting her first-aid kit to a more comfortable carrying position. "Not many cars pass on the road at this time of day. The distance is much longer."

"We can dog-trot part of it," Judy said, beginning to lope along. "Anyway, we're well out ahead of the others!"

"I can see another group starting out," Beverly reported looking back. "They chose the short, hard way."

"Since we're out ahead, that might be their only chance to beat us," Betty reasoned. "I still think we chose the better, faster route."

Alternately, the girls dog-trotted twenty steps and then walked the same number. In that manner, they did not tire so easily or lose breath.

The road wound on through the forest in dips and sharp ascents. They kept going, ignoring the heat of the sun and their own increasing weariness.

"I'm glad we didn't take the hard climb," Judy commented as she and Kathleen paused a moment to wait for Betty and Beverly to catch up. "The going will be tough enough before we reach Hermit's Ridge."

At the next sharp bend in the highway, the Scouts were able to look down at the table top some distance below. Not a single patrol seemed to have followed them.

"I knew it!" Beverly exclaimed. "All the others have taken the shorter routes!"

"Let them," Judy replied cheerfully. "It hasn't

been proven yet that our judgment was poor. We've been making fast time."

"We haven't caught that ride yet," Beverly reminded her. "Not a single car has passed us on the road. And we've met only one truck."

Resting only momentarily, the four went on, doggedly determined to be the first to reach Hermit's Ridge. Soon they lost all view of their competitors who had been swallowed up by the dense forest foliage.

"Say, I think I hear a truck coming now!" Betty presently exclaimed. She paused to cock an attentive ear. "Wow! It's coming fast, burning up the road!"

"We'll never flag down that driver!" Judy exclaimed, moving hastily off the pavement.

The heavy freight carrier roared past the girls, its massive tires screaming as it went around a bend.

"What does that driver think this road is—a speedway?" Beverly demanded. "Why, it's dangerous—"

The four hikers halted abruptly, frozen by the fearful sound of screeching brakes. They could not see beyond the next sharp curve, but the sickening thud was unmistakable. The speeding truck had missed its turn and had skidded off the road!

Chapter 8

VALUABLE CARGO

ROUNDING the bend at a run, the four Scouts saw that the big truck had missed plunging over the ravine by mere inches.

The heavily loaded vehicle had skidded wildly, bringing up at a sharp angle against a rocky embankment. Shattered glass lay on the pavement.

Judy was the first to reach the tilted truck cab. She could not at first get the jammed door open, but suddenly it gave, swinging back so hard, she nearly was thrown off balance.

The driver was slumped over the wheel, stunned and bleeding from flesh cuts. He was a heavy-set man with a beak-like nose and square jaw which sagged to give him a stupid appearance. His eyes were glazed and unseeing.

The only other occupant of the truck, a thin man with two front teeth missing, sprawled half off the seat, moaning and using foul language.

"My neck!" he screamed. "It's like killing me! Don't stand there! Do something! Get a doctor!"

He pulled himself out of the cab, pushing angrily at Kathleen when she tried to help him. Despite the rebuff she took his arm to steady him.

VALUABLE CARGO 71

"Don't touch me! Get away!" he screamed, staggering. Kathleen caught a whiff of his breath then and knew that he had been drinking. She noted that his right arm hung limp and that the right shoulder was much lower than the left. He had grasped it at the elbow to provide support.

"You can't raise your arm above your shoulder, can you?" she demanded. "Your collar bone must be fractured."

"So what?" the trucker demanded savagely. He leaned weakly against the truck, ignoring her efforts to be of help.

Meanwhile, Judy, Beverly and Betty had devoted their attention to the truck driver, who appeared in more serious condition than the disagreeable passenger.

Carefully, they stretched him out flat on the cab seat.

"He may be only stunned," Judy said anxiously. "The first thing is to get the blood stopped. No artery has been cut fortunately."

The blood came from two facial cuts and a wrist which had been slashed by flying glass. Judy removed a tiny splinter of glass from the latter wound, treated the cut with antiseptic, placed a compress over the opening and bandaged it tightly.

That job done, the girls bandaged the driver's face, noting with relief that he seemed to be recovering from shock. Now and then he moaned in pain as they worked deftly and efficiently, but for the most part he eyed them silently.

Kathleen, on the other hand, was having a most trying time with her patient, who refused to cooperate. He would not lie down or let her examine his neck.

"I can't do anything with him," she whispered to Judy. "I'm sure he has a fractured collar bone. But what to do about it? He's acting like a maniac."

"Delirious?"

"He's just a mean character," Kathleen muttered in an undertone. "I'm sort of scared."

"Scared? Why?"

"He has a revolver in his back pocket."

"Maybe he carries it to protect the cargo," Judy replied. "Let's see what we can do about that collar bone."

Moving over to the sullen trucker, who stood leaning against the tilted vehicle, she adressed him quietly but firmly.

"You'll feel more comfortable if you sit or lie down. We'll help you—"

"I don't want any help." The trucker's lips parted in an ugly snarl which revealed his missing front teeth. "You got a car?"

"No, we're Girl Scouts on a hike."

"Girl Scouts! A lot of help you'll be!"

Judy ignored the sarcasm, noting how limply the trucker's right arm hung.

"We can help," she insisted. "Your collar bone has been broken, I think."

"So what?" the trucker demanded belligerently. "I'm worried about this truck. We can never move it out of this—have to abandon it."

"You should be able to get a wrecker from the village. Now about that collar bone—"

"Forget it, I said." The man's gaze roved toward the cab of the truck where Betty and Beverly were covering the driver with coats.

"Is Joe done for?" he demanded with cold rather than friendly concern.

"He's more stunned than hurt, I think," Judy replied.

"Can't he make it on his own pins? We gotta get out o' here."

"He shouldn't try to walk. We'll bring help to you as fast as we can. First, though, you must take a sensible attitude and let us wrap that collar bone. You'll be far more comfortable until we can get you a doctor."

"Okay," the trucker suddenly consented. "Make it snappy though, and don't hurt me' or I'll bash you in! I ain't in no mood to be worked over by amateurs."

Having cajoled the man into a more cooperative mood, Judy went quickly to work. With Kathleen helping, she utilized a triangular bandage as a sling for the right arm, tying it snugly to the side of his body with a cravat bandage.

accident and of the strange behavior of the truckers who had rejected assistance.

"Did you notice the license number of the truck?" one of the highway patrolmen asked.

None of the Scouts had made a note of it.

"We were too busy wrapping up wounds to think of that," Judy confessed.

The patrolmen next inquired if the girls could describe the two truckers.

"Oh, yes!" Kathleen said eagerly. "The passenger was a thin fellow with two teeth missing. He had dark bushy eyebrows and was very disagreeable."

"That was Ben Vodner, I'll bet a cent!" one of the patrolmen exclaimed. "Did he have a scar on his left cheek?"

"Yes, he did!" Judy recalled. "A long jagged white mark!"

"What did the other man look like?"

"His most prominent feature was a large hooked nose," Judy described him. "He was a large man, heavy-set and with a square jaw. I'd say he weighed about two hundred pounds—"

"That's Joe Pompilli for sure!"

"Who is he?" Kathleen demanded.

"Joe's the ring leader of a bunch of hi-jackers," one of the patrolmen informed her. "Off and on for the last six months, he and his boys have been hi-jacking cargo and taking it through here right under the noses of the forest rangers."

"So that was why they didn't want help!" Judy

VALUABLE CARGO

exclaimed. "That truck that went off the road was loaded with stolen cargo!"

"Tires snatched from the Graystone Transport Co. The truck was held up early this morning across the state line."

Taking the girls into the patrol car, the two patrolmen proceeded with all speed toward the scene of the accident.

"It's just around the next bend," Judy informed the driver.

"Then I'll let you girls out here," he said, pulling up at the side of the road. "There may be shooting. Stay back until we see what's what."

Piling out of the car, the Scouts waited until the patrolmen had driven on. Then, they rounded the bend, tense and expectant.

The truck remained in the ditch where last they had seen it, but neither of the injured men were anywhere visible.

Watching from a safe distance, the girls saw the patrolmen carefully search the truck cab.

"Those two hi-jackers have fled!" Judy exclaimed. "I guess they weren't as badly hurt as we thought!"

At a run, the Scouts raced up the road to join the patrolmen, who by this time had broken open the door lock on the back of the truck.

"Just as I thought," one of the searchers declared as he swung open the double doors. "Stolen auto tires!"

Judy and her friends were bewildered with re-

wide berth for awhile," the other patrolman added. "You never can tell though."

"That's right," agreed George Franey. "They're daring outlaws, well organized. Joe Pompilli won't abandon this run because of one mishap. But we'll be watching for him!"

As was to be expected, Judy, Beverly, Betty and Kathleen, were regarded somewhat as heroines by their camp mates. Many times they were called upon to recite their adventures on the lonely mountain road.

"We've given a bandage-by-bandage report so many times I'm beginning to embellish the details," Judy laughed as she told the story for perhaps the twelfth time. "That thin fellow the patrolmen called Ben was a mean sort of individual. He didn't actually threaten us with his gun though."

"The worst of it was that we lost out in the Hermit Ridge competition," added Kathleen ruefully. "I'm afraid we'll have to depend on Ardeth and Virginia to win points for our patrol."

She smiled at the other two, who had spent most of the morning searching for a suitable specimen to add to the nature treasure chest.

Both girls were sunburned and discouraged. True, they had captured an unwary bull frog and a rare type of water insect, but only to learn that other units had made similar entries during their absence from camp.

"So now to qualify, we'll have to find something different," Ardeth asserted. "I'm sick about it."

"Oh, we'll get an entry before the deadline," Judy said cheerfully.

"We have several days to work on it," added Kathleen.

"The other campers have combed the lake and the area around here so thoroughly that it will be hard to find anything unusual," Ardeth insisted with a shake of her head. "All of the common things such as worms, bugs, and bees, have been used too!"

"Maybe we can find an entry while we're at Calico Cottage," Kathleen suggested. "The woods near the cave haven't been explored."

"We might enter the Cottage ghost!" Judy said with a chuckle. "If we could capture him, we'd be entitled to first prize!"

"By the way, have you heard from your aunt?" Ardeth inquired.

Judy nodded and displayed a telegram which she carried in her pocket. "This came in the morning delivery from town," she explained. "Aunt Mattie will arrive on the 2:10 p.m. train tomorrow."

"Have you told her about the cottage having a ghost?"

"No, and I'm not eager to either," Judy returned with a grimace. "Aunt Mattie might make a dreadful fuss. I wish we could clear up the mystery before she gets here."

"We have tonight to work on it," Kathleen remarked thoughtfully. "If only we could get down into the cottage basement! It wouldn't do though, to break the door lock."

"Hardly," Judy agreed. "Mr. Krumm would have a just complaint then!"

Though the Beaver Patrol girls made light of the "ghost" and the strange flute music which had disturbed their slumbers at the cottage, they were determined to find a logical explanation for the occurrence.

Judy and her friends had said very little about the mysterious happening, but the story had leaked out and greatly enlarged in the telling. Throughout the afternoon, the girls were besieged by questions. Their rivals in the Lone Tree unit seemed especially interested.

"We're certainly the target of attention," Judy remarked to Kathleen. "I can't understand why the Lone Tree girls are so fascinated by every detail. Something's in the wind!"

The Beaver Patrol members remained at camp for dinner and to enjoy a ceremonial camp fire which wound up with the telling of ghost stories. At nine o'clock, the station wagon took Judy, Kathleen, Miss Ward, Ardeth and Virginia to Calico Cottage for the night.

"We'll have our tent by tomorrow, I'm quite sure," Miss Ward told the girls as they let themselves into the dark cottage. "That will be a relief."

"I don't mind being here," Virginia asserted. "In fact, I think it's exciting! Do you suppose we'll hear that flute player tonight?"

"We will if we keep dwelling upon it," Miss Ward replied as she switched on the lights. "The mind, you know, plays strange tricks. Now everyone to bed, and no nonsense."

Rather soberly, the girls went to their rooms. Because Miss Ward was with them, they had no fear of spending a night in the cottage. Nevertheless, they were somewhat tense with expectancy.

Ardeth was removing a shoe, when suddenly she stiffened. "Listen!" she directed. "What was that?"

"I heard nothing," returned Virginia.

"I thought I heard a thumping sound in the cellar," Ardeth insisted in a hushed voice.

"That was your own heart pounding, goose!" teased Kathleen. "Jump into bed, and stop imagining things."

Ardeth obediently turned off the bedroom light. Going to the window, she opened it, and stood for a moment, gazing toward the dark forest which edged ominously close to the cottage lawn.

"Kathleen! Virginia!" she summoned the others, drawing in her breath.

"Now what?" Kathleen demanded.

"Come here, quick! Tell me what you see." Dramatically, Ardeth pointed toward the towering trees.

Virginia went quickly to the window, peering in

the direction indicated. She stood silent and tense, scarcely believing her own eyesight.

"It's—it's something white, and it moves!" she exclaimed.

Kathleen had joined the other two. Ardeth gripped her hand so tightly it hurt. "I'm scared," she confessed shakely. "What do you think, Kathy?"

"I'll call Miss Ward and Judy."

Quickly, she summoned the other two from the next bedroom. Neither had started to disrobe for the night. For several minutes the five stood at the darkened window, gazing out across the sloping lawn to the dark backdrop of trees.

Plainly they could see a white object moving lazily back and forth against a curtain of foliage. A nearly full moon added to the eerie effect, casting a ghostly light over the lonely forest area.

"A spook!" Ardeth declared shakily. "It's coming this way too!"

"No such thing," Miss Ward corrected in a firm voice. "Whatever the object may be, it is not moving in this direction. I'll get my flashlight and investigate."

"I'll go with you," Judy offered.

Putting on warm jackets, the two slipped out of the cottage. The night was chilly, for a light breeze blew from the direction of the river.

Judy and the teacher focussed their eyes on the white object at the edge of the woods. Though it continued to move lazily, its basic position did not seem to change.

"Keep well behind me, Judy," Miss Ward directed as they drew near the trees. "I doubt that there is any serious cause for alarm, but it's wise to proceed cautiously."

Having decided upon a bold approach, the pair moved directly toward the white object.

When they were within a few yards of it, Miss Ward switched on the flashlight. She directed the beam squarely upon the fluttering "ghost."

"Why, it looks like a bed sheet!" Judy exclaimed, and burst into relieved laughter.

"A sheet attached to a bush!" added Miss Ward. "Let's find out about this."

She held the light while Judy removed the sheet from the foliage. To prevent it from blowing away, two ends had been tied to the branches with cord.

"This 'ghost' was put here purposely!" Judy declared. "By whom, I wonder?"

"Any marking on the linen?"

Judy inspected the sheet under the light. "Here are some initials stamped on the edge!" she exclaimed. 'P.C.C.'"

"Pine Cone Camp!"

"Well, if that isn't a good joke on us!" Judy laughed. "The girls at camp decided to produce that ghost we were telling them about! Beverly and Betty may have pulled this one!"

"They were in camp all afternoon, Judy."

"That's true. Maybe some of the Lone Tree Scouts did it then! One of their girls has been asking a lot of questions about Calico Cottage."

"I don't mind a bit of good fun," Miss Ward said, folding the sheet. "On the other hand, I'm not in favor of making too much of this ghost talk. I think I'll discuss the matter with Miss Lubell tomorrow."

"I hope whoever played the trick won't get into trouble. I'm sure it was all in good fun."

"Oh, no one will receive a reprimand," Miss Ward promised. "I'll find out which girls had camp leave this afternoon. If it develops that any of them played the trick, I'll ask them not to repeat it, that's all."

When the two returned to the cottage with the bed sheet, Virginia, Ardeth and Kathleen anxiously met them at the door.

"Here's your ghost!" Judy laughed, tossing the camp linen into Kathleen's arms. "Look at the initials!"

"So that's why those Lone Tree Scouts were giggling and carrying on this afternoon!" Kathleen exclaimed after she had examined the markings. "Several of them asked for camp leave too!"

"Then my idea about that probably was right," Miss Ward said.

Greatly relieved that the ghost scare had no serious aspects, the Scouts discussed the prank for a few minutes, and then went to bed. It was a long while, however, before the house finally settled down.

Judy fell quickly asleep. How long she slumbered she had no way of knowing. But suddenly, she found herself wide awake.

Miss Ward, she noted, was sleeping soundly beside her.

Wondering what had disturbed her, Judy sat up. Moonlight streamed into the bedroom. She judged that it could not be later than midnight or possibly one o'clock.

The telephone was ringing.

"So that's what awakened me!" Judy thought, leaping out of bed. "Wonder who can be calling at this time of night?"

The phone call, she thought, might be from Pine Cone Camp. Something might have happened to Betty or Beverly. Or possibly it was a message from Aunt Mattie.

In her haste to reach the telephone before it stopped ringing, Judy bumped against a chair. Nursing a bruised knee, she hobbled on.

As she took down the receiver to say "hello," a gruff voice came over the line.

"Time you answered! Is Joe there?"

"Joe?" faltered Judy. "Joe who?"

Only silence gave reply. Then the wire went completely dead. The speaker at the other end of the line had hung up.

Chapter 10

A MIDNIGHT DISTURBANCE

AS JUDY hung up the telephone receiver, the light suddenly was switched on behind her. Startled, she whirled around with a smothered exclamation of alarm.

"I didn't mean to frighten you, Judy." It was Kathleen who stood in the doorway, a corduroy robe flung over her shoulders. "I heard someone moving around, and thought I'd check, that's all. Is anything wrong?"

"The phone was ringing. I—I don't know what to make of it."

"Who was it that called, Judy?"

"That's the point. I don't know. Someone asked for Joe."

"Joe? Joe who?"

"That's exactly what I asked, Kathleen. The only Joe I know is that dreadful Joe Pompilli."

"Someone must have called the wrong number."

"I guess so," Judy admitted doubtfully. "It gave me an ugly start though. What time is it?"

"A little past midnight," Kathleen said, looking at her wristwatch. "What a night! All we need to make it complete is a little flute music!"

A MIDNIGHT DISTURBANCE   89

The switching on of a light had disturbed the others in the cottage. Miss Ward came in from the bedroom and then Virginia and Ardeth, the latter groggy with sleep.

"What now?" she mumbled. "Another ghost?"

Judy explained about the telephone.

"Those Lone Tree Scouts!" Virginia exclaimed indignantly. "They're playing another joke on us! Trying to pretend that Joe Pompilli is calling!"

"It wasn't anyone from Pine Cone Camp," Judy said, her face serious. "Whoever called was a man."

"It must have been someone who dialed a wrong number," Kathleen insisted. "I'm in favor of forgetting the whole business, and going to bed. If we don't get some sleep we'll all be wrecks tomorrow."

"That's sound advice," approved Miss Ward. "To bed everyone!"

All the girls were up at seven o'clock the next morning, feeling little the worse for the excitement of the night. While the Scouts were washing the breakfast dishes, the telephone rang again.

"You get it, Judy," Virginia directed with a giggle. "It's probably from Joe."

"From Aunt Mattie more than likely," Judy replied, moving hastily to the telephone.

The message was from Miss Lubell at Pine Cone Camp. She asked Judy to tell Miss Ward that the station wagon driver had been delayed that morning and could not call for the girls until ten thirty.

"This means we'll have considerable free time on our hands," Judy remarked as she relayed the information to the others.

"Let's explore the river area, and maybe around the cave," proposed Ardeth. "I want to find an insect or an animal we can enter in the nature treasure chest."

"We'll all go," Miss Ward decided.

The work already had been finished. Locking the cottage, the five struck off down the private road. After it dead-ended, they went on across the silvery-gray rocks and through a stretch of sand to the river.

Beyond the ribbon of blue water, the mountains rose in jagged green peaks. A ranger station was visible on one of the high slopes, set in a cleared area among the trees.

A half-rotted dock extended for some distance out into the stream. The girls noticed an elderly man in blue overalls tying up his rowboat after a fishing expedition.

"Good morning," Judy said pleasantly as the girls wandered over. "How's the fishing?"

Straightening up, the old man shoved a soiled white cap at a rakish angle over his shaggy white hair.

" Mornin' to you," he greeted the girls jovially. "The fishin'? Nary a bite! Blast my timbers, it's a waste of a man's time to blister his skin out in the sun on this old river. I'm slingin' my hook for today."

Moving stiffly, the elderly man began to unload his fishing equipment from the boat. Judy and Kathleen reached down to help him.

"Right handy mates ye be," he remarked, well pleased by their attention. "Don't recollect seein' you gals hereabouts before. Tourists?"

"We're Girl Scouts," Judy explained. "We're staying at Pine Cone Camp. Because of a mix-up there over reservations, some of us have been sleeping at Calico Cottage."

"Calico Cottage? Well, bash my binnacles!"

"It's a lovely cottage," Ardeth contributed. "The only trouble is, it seems to have a ghost."

"A musical ghost who plays a flute at night," added Virginia.

"You don't say! A ghost!" The old man gave a throaty chuckle and then laughed so hard that his sizeable stomach rolled up and down under the overalls. "I'll be a son of a sea cook! That's a good joke on Krumm!"

"It's not so much fun for us though," Judy declared earnestly. "We're turning the cottage over to my aunt this afternoon. She's inclined to be nervous. We'd hoped to clear up the mystery before she arrived, but that seems out of the question now."

"Don't waste any time worrying about that ghost," the old man advised. "A bunch o' Girl Scouts ought to be smart enough to get to wind'ard of any flute-playin' spook."

"It would seem that way," agreed Judy. "So far, though, we've had no luck. By the way, you're not Captain Hager by any chance?"

"That's my name, but not by chance! Captain Humphrey Hager, formerly master of the good ship *Elaine*. I've been in dry dock going on ten years now."

"We're glad to meet you," Judy declared cordially. She introduced Miss Ward and the girls, and then added: "Bart Ranieau told us that you once owned Calico Cottage—or rather, the old homestead that stood on the same foundation."

"That's right," Old Captain Hager agreed, his leathery face wrinkling into a scowl. "I found myself in low water, financially speaking. That blasted, penny-squeezin' Krumm kept pestering me, until finally I sold him the place."

"Tell us, Captain Hager," urged Kathleen, "did the house have a ghost when you lived there?"

A knowing smile overspread the old man's face. "Well, yes, and no," he said. "I advised Krumm to put in a new foundation, but he let me know he would do it his own way. So now he has a ghost! Ha!"

"Does the old foundation have anything to do with the ghost?" Virginia asked, looking puzzled.

Old Captain Hager acted as if he had not heard

the question. He fussed with the painter of the rowboat for a moment, and then remarked offhand:

"So you gals have met Bart Ranieau? Now there's a fine lad, smart as a whip and with the courage of a young lion. He told you about Hager's Hole?"

"Calico Cave?" inquired Judy.

"Hager's Hole," the old man repeated. "I don't take stock of that new fancy name Krumm tacked on. Bart told you about his father losing his life in the cave?"

"Why no!" exclaimed Judy.

"He did say something about an explorer trying to find the cave's exit, and never being heard of again," Virginia added.

"That was Bart's father," the Captain informed her. "His son's a chip off the old block. Lots of sand in the craw! Bart's trying to work his way through college by peddlin' milk. Aye, he's an up and comer!"

"How did Bart's father lose his life?" Miss Ward inquired.

The old captain's gaze swept the river and lifted to fasten thoughtfully upon the dark entranceway of Calico Cave.

"No one knows," he replied. "Not for sure. Folks say though, that it was the siphon that did for him."

"What's a siphon?" demanded Kathleen.

"Hager's Hole has an underground river," he related. "Where it empties no one knows. Deep in

Chapter 11

SPELL OF THE CAVE

CAPTAIN Hager's remarks about the cave had stirred the imagination of the Scouts, and even Miss Ward thought it would be interesting to explore the cavern for a short distance.

"Would it be safe, do you think?" she asked, as Captain Hager seemed to be giving Judy's request sober consideration.

"It's safe enough, Ma'am," he assured her. "The only danger lies in going too far without a guide."

"No rock falls?"

"Never heard of one in all the years I've lived hereabouts."

"Then do take us, Captain Hager!" Judy urged again, prancing excitedly about the dock. "We haven't much time, because the camp station wagon is to come for us at ten thirty. Please, could we start right now?"

"Dash it, I was calculatin' on anchorin' for a comfortable snooze," the captain complained good-naturedly. "But if them's my sailing orders, we'll cast off for the cave!"

The old man told the Scouts and their leader to meet him at the entranceway of Hager's Hole. He promised to join them there as soon as he had gone to his nearby river shack to leave his fishing equipment and pick up a few items he would want for the trip.

Taking leave of the old man, the girls swiftly climbed the slope to the cave. Captain Hager did not keep them waiting long.

Within fifteen minutes, they glimpsed his bent figure coming along the path. He had changed his shoes, put on a blue jacket, and carried a lantern.

Before leading the way into the cave, Captain Hager told the group something of its history. The cavern, he related, was known to have been in existence in early Indian days—the exact date of its origin never would be established.

"Now there are all types of caves," he went on, warming to his subject. "Tunnel caves, river system caves, fissure caves—no two ever are the same, and that's what makes 'em so interesting to explorers. This one starts with a sort of sinkhole entrance. It narrows down for a distance and then opens up into a chamber where you'll see the White Witch. That's as far as most folks ever go."

"It won't take us too long to see the formation?" Miss Ward asked, looking anxiously at her wrist watch. "We haven't much time."

"Ten minutes, ma'am, to walk to the chamber. The climb back will take longer. I'm not as spry as I was in the old day."

"We can spare an hour," Miss Ward decided.

Captain Hager instructed the girls to follow him, single-file. Miss Ward brought up the rear of the procession to make certain that none of her charges wandered out of line.

Cautiously, and with awe, the Scouts moved into the entrance chamber of the cave. A considerable current of air moved in the cavern, nearly lifting Kathleen's beret from her head.

The room in which the girls found themselves, though dark, was neither damp nor musty. By the light of Captain Hager's lantern, they distinguished smoke-blackened limestone walls, and on the floor were the dead ashes of a small fire.

"Someone has been in here lately," the guide remarked. "Not Bart, because he wouldn't bother with a fire. He does most of his exploring in a bathing suit."

"A bathing suit!" gasped Miss Ward, truly astonished. "I should think he'd freeze to death."

"Not that lad," chuckled the captain. He had rested his lantern for a moment on a rocky ledge. "The temperature of this cave is the same, summer or winter. Bart wears a bathing suit because he can crawl through narrow places better than if he had on bulky clothes. And when he gets wet, he says he stays warmer and dries out faster."

"Dear me, there's more to this exploration of caves than I realized," commented Miss Ward. "We'll not get wet, I trust.?"

"No, Ma'am," the captain promised. "There's no

SPELL OF THE CAVE

water down to the level where we're going. Keep your eyes out for bats though—not that the little creatures will harm you."

"Bats!" Virginia squealed. "Horrors!"

"They won't hurt you," the captain repeated. "Not even if you touch 'em with your hand. Sometimes they're packed in on the walls as tight as a swarm o' bees. Then if they're disturbed, the whole mass may take flight. Bats are strange creatures."

"Ardeth should be assigned to capture one for the camp treasure chest!" Judy chuckled.

"We'll go below, now," the captain announced. "Follow me closely, and don't do too much talkin'. Sound echoes in a cave and is magnified. Full steam ahead!"

Step by step, the Scouts descended the narrow passageway. The slope was an easy one, but it seemed endless. Unable to judge distance underground, the girls imagined they had gone a long ways when finally the captain brought up in a gallery approximately sixteen feet wide.

Walls of the room were covered with limestone ridges and there were a few interesting stalagmites and stalactites. Captain Hager struck one of the latter with his stout walking stick, and it gave forth a musical ring.

Waiting until the entire party had clustered about, he slowly moved his lantern so that it threw a circular, shadowy light on a dark portion of the gallery.

The girls sucked in their breath, uttering exclamations of surprise and awe.

There before them, was the cave witch!

Tall and skinny, she appeared to lean on a long, white staff. The ice-like figure, the girls knew, had been formed by stalagmites and stalactites which over the years had grown together in weird formation.

For a long while they stood silent, held by the ghostly spell of the old witch. In the dead stillness, they could hear the rush of the mysterious hidden river far below them. A cold gust of air blew across the gallery, causing the Scouts to pull their jackets more closely about them.

"How real that old witch looks!" Judy whispered, finally breaking the silence. "No wonder folks make up tales about this cave."

Keeping his voice low to prevent echo, Captain Hager explained that the dripstone formations were called stalactites when they hung from the limestone ceiling and stalagmites if they rose from the cave floor.

"Each icicle-like formation, if broken, shows growth rings not unlike those of a tree," he related. Some, he told the Scouts, grew very rapidly, while others were years in the making.

"Usually each stalactite has a small hole in the center through which the water flows to drip off the end," he went on. "When the drip-off strikes the floor, it sometimes builds up a stalagmite as you see

SPELL OF THE CAVE 101

them here. When the two unite, you may get any variety of weird shapes."

"Oh, dear," protested Kathleen, "you're taking all the magic away from the White Witch, Captain Hager! I prefer to imagine that she is pure white stone."

Virginia inquired if there were other interesting formations deeper down in the cave.

"Aye, in the gallery below, there's one Bart calls the Grand Ballroom. Farther on, there's a Frozen Waterfall, or flowstone, as it's called. You can see needles and toadstools and totem poles."

"Oh, Captain Hager, take us on!" pleaded Ardeth. "Only as far as the Ballroom. This cave is so fascinating."

Before the captain could answer, Miss Ward interposed firmly: "No, girls. Perhaps some other day, if we have a guide, we can return."

"The camp station wagon will be at Calico Cottage before we are, if we don't hurry," declared Kathleen. "This is such a wonderful grotto, I hate to leave, but we must."

Regretfully, the others agreed that further exploration of the cave must be postponed. Leading the way with the lantern, Captain Hager began the steep climb. He moved slowly and in the narrow passageway, his heavy breathing was so loud that those behind him could hear it plainly.

"I'm not as spry as I was ten years ago," the old man confessed when the party presently reached the cave exit. "Going down is easy enough, but when I throw 'er in reverse, my ticker starts to pound."

"We shouldn't have pressed you into taking us to see the old witch," Judy apologized.

"I was glad to do it," the captain insisted. "Anyway, I'm not ready yet to let old age get to the windward of me! No, sir!"

The Scouts thanked their guide for taking them on the expedition. Saying goodbye, they hastened along the rocky path to the private road, thence to Calico Cottage. To their relief, the camp station wagon had not yet arrived.

"What a wonderful morning!" Kathleen declared, sitting down on the porch steps to think over the exciting things she had seen inside the cave. "I wish all the girls at Pine Cone Camp could see the White Witch!"

"Perhaps it can be arranged," Miss Ward remarked. "I'll talk to Miss Lubell about it and see what she thinks. Caves certainly are educational."

"Captain Hager knows a lot about them too," contributed Judy. "He told us a great deal, but I have a hunch there's more he left unsaid."

"About the White Witch?" inquired Virginia.

"The White Witch and maybe some other things," she hinted. "Both Captain Hager and Bart seem to dislike Mr. Krumm. If it weren't for that personal feeling, I suspect they might tell us more about the ghost of Calico Cottage."

Chapter 12

THE PRIVATE ROAD

AFTER lunch at Pine Top Camp, the Scouts busied themselves washing their clothes and cleaning the Beaver Patrol tent. Miss Lubell sent word by one of the counselors that other quarters would be available for the girls by nightfall.

"I guess we'll have no excuse for staying at Calico Cottage tonight," Judy said regretfully. "You know, that boy with the flute intrigues me!"

"Everyone in camp has heard about him," added Ardeth as she hung a blouse on the line to dry. "We're being teased no end. If we don't solve the mystery before we leave here, we'll never hear the last of it."

Miss Ward had overheard the conversation, and interposed a word. "It might be well for a couple of Scouts to stay with Judy's aunt tonight," she proposed. "I'm satisfied that the cottage is safe, but strange sounds at night can be most disturbing to a nervous person alone."

"I'll stay with Aunt Mattie, if I may," Judy promptly volunteered.

"I'd like to myself," added Ardeth. "While I'm there, I want to visit the cave again. If I could get one of those bats we heard about, we'd have a fine entry for the nature treasure chest."

"The cave is out-of-bounds without a guide," Miss Ward returned. "I talked to Miss Lubell about it. She thinks we may be able to arrange a tour for the entire camp later this week. The problem is to find a suitable guide. It seems that with the exception of Bart and Captain Hager, few persons go near the place."

"Someone has been in there lately," Judy said, reminding the teacher of the dead camp fire ashes they had seen at the cave entrance.

Shortly before two o'clock, the station wagon took Miss Ward, Judy and Ardeth to the village depot. A smoky haze hung over the mountainside, and the girls were somewhat disturbed to learn that a small forest fire had broken out across the river on Brady's Ridge.

Enroute to the station they met a forest service truck and passed a ranger with a portable radio on his shoulder.

The driver of the station wagon pulled up, to ask the forest service man if the situation was considered at all serious.

"Everything's under control," the ranger assured him. "It's a small brush fire. We're keeping a close watch of the entire area though."

"How did the fire start?" inquired Miss Ward.

The ranger shrugged. "Perhaps from a carelessly dropped cigarette. Or a motorist may have tossed a match out of a car window. The fire apparently started close to the road. You folks will be all right, if you don't try to cross the river. Keep on this side."

The haze of smoke hung low as the station wagon parked near the depot. Judy sniffed the fumes and coughed.

"What a welcome for Aunt Mattie!" she remarked. "She'll be scared to death that the fire will spread to this side of the river. And if we tell her about the ghost—"

"I don't believe I'd do that," Miss Ward advised. "At least not for a day or so. Why disturb her unnecessarily?"

"You're right," Judy promptly agreed. "If the ghost makes any more trouble, Aunt Mattie will find out about it soon enough. Mum's the word."

The train proved to be half an hour late. Finally it rumbled in, throwing up dust and cinders. Aunt Mattie Meadows was on the last Pullman car. She was a jolly-faced woman of forty-two, well turned out in a trim gray suit, with a white carnation in the lapel.

"Hi, Aunt Mattie!" Judy cried, rushing to greet her.

Miss Meadows enfolded her niece in a warm embrace, and then held her off at arm's length for a better view.

"Why, you're brown as an Indian!" she exclaimed. "What have you done to your complexion?"

"Liberal doses of sun, wind and lake water," Judy

chuckled. She turned to present Miss Ward and Ardeth.

Miss Meadows greeted them, made a few casual remarks and then sniffed the air. "Goodness! Do I smell smoke?" she demanded. "Is something on fire?"

"Only a little brush across the river," Judy said carelessly. She picked up her aunt's suitcase and started for the station wagon. "Nothing to worry about."

Aunt Mattie kept sniffing the air. "Dear me, it doesn't seem a little fire could make so much smoke. Judy, are you quite sure there's no danger? You're not keeping anything from me?"

"The ranger assured us there is no danger. Don't give it a thought, Aunt Mattie."

Miss Meadows fell silent as she was escorted to the waiting station wagon. Nevertheless, she kept gazing toward the horizon in the direction of the river.

Going up the winding mountain road, the woman became increasingly ill at ease. At each sharp turn, she instinctively braced herself, as if fearing the car would roll off into a ravine.

"I hope you rented a nice cottage for me, Judy," she chatted. "You didn't write me a word about it."

"There wasn't time, Aunt Mattie. In fact, we didn't have any choice in selecting the cottage. We had to take the only place available."

"Is it a quiet place? I've had a hard, tiring year, and I do want to have complete rest."

"Well, Calico Cottage is off the beaten path," Judy replied evasively. "How quiet it will prove to be no one can predict."

The station wagon rounded a curve and slowed to a standstill. Peering ahead, the girls saw that a wooden barrier had been placed across part of the highway, blocking traffic.

"Now what?" murmured Judy. "This wasn't here when we came down the mountain an hour ago."

A state highway patrolman came over to the station wagon. Recognizing the driver and the occupants, he told them they might proceed.

"We're checking every car," he told the group. "We have a report some hi-jackers, who took a truck at Oelwein, are coming this way. With the forest service tied up fighting a forest fire, and most of our men helping 'em, they probably figured they could slip a cargo through."

"Hi-jackers!" Aunt Mattie exclaimed in dismay. "Judy, what sort of a place is this?"

"Never a dull moment," Judy responded lightly. "You'll love it here!"

"Judy, tell her about your meeting with Joe—" Ardeth began, only to let her voice trail off as Miss Ward directed a warning glance in her direction.

The station wagon moved on past the barrier and drew up presently at Calico Cottage. Aunt Mattie, who had fallen into a weary silence, suddenly revived at sight of the little house.

"Why, it's charming!" she cried. "Judy, you couldn't have found a nicer place. So peaceful looking, set back among the trees."

"Let's hope Calico Cottage lives up to its appearance," Judy said, leading the way across the lawn. "Ardeth and I thought we'd stay with you tonight, so you won't be lonesome. Do you mind?"

"I'll be happy to have you! I'm not afraid to stay alone at night, but I'll admit I'll rest easier with someone in the house. Especially with a forest fire burning at my doorstep, and hi-jackers on the main highway!"

"It's not that bad," Judy protested.

After seeing that Miss Meadows was comfortably settled in the cottage, Miss Ward decided to return with the station wagon driver to Pine Cone Camp. Before leaving, she talked privately with Judy.

"Everything should be all right here," she said, "but if by chance anything does go wrong, call me at once."

"We'll be safe and comfortable," Judy insisted. "No more ghost scares I hope."

"Miss Lubell put a stop to that," the teacher informed her. "We checked and learned that it was the Lone Tree girls who attached the bed sheet to the bushes. They've promised not to pull any more tricks."

After the station wagon had departed, Judy and

Ardeth helped Miss Meadows unpack. Her enthusiasm for the cottage was boundless. She was especially delighted with the kitchen and went about poking in the high cupboards over the sink.

"Tomorrow when I am rested, I'll straighten all the dishes and rearrange them more to my liking." she announced. "I never feel that I'm settled in a place until I've cleaned the cupboards."

With the supplies on hand, Aunt Mattie cooked a magnificent supper, topping it off with biscuits and a custard pie. The meal finished, she suddenly collapsed from weariness, leaving the dishes for Judy and Ardeth.

"I declare, I don't know what's come over me," she apologized. "The long train ride must have worn me out. I can't keep my eyes open."

"Go straight to bed, Aunt Mattie. Ardeth and I will take care of everything."

"I believe I will turn in," Miss Meadows said, covering a yawn. "You'll be sure to lock all the doors?"

"Every one," Judy promised.

The sink was fairly loaded with dishes, for Aunt Mattie did not skimp on them when she cooked a meal. After scouring the last stubborn pan, Judy hung up the dish rag with a tired sigh.

"Shall we turn in?" she asked Ardeth.

"We may as well, I guess. Wonder what the girls are doing at Pine Cone?"

"Singing songs and telling stories by the camp fire, like as not. Wish you were there, Ardeth?"

"Someone should stay here this first night with your aunt. I don't mind, Judy. Do you suppose—"

"We'll have a serenade from our friend with the flute?" Judy supplied. "For Aunt Mattie's sake I hope not. If she hears about a ghost on top of hijackers and a forest fire, she's likely to pack her suitcase and leave."

Ardeth had moved to the open kitchen door. "There isn't as much smoke in the air now," she reported. "Either the wind is carrying it the other direction, or the fire has died down."

After closing the windows and making certain the doors were locked, the two girls presently went to their bedroom which adjoined the one Miss Meadows had taken.

Judy secretly had made up her mind she would lie awake a long while to be sure that nothing went amiss in the cottage. However, her bed was so pleasantly comfortable, that despite her firm resolution, she dozed off almost at once.

When finally she awakened, it was to find herself being shaken by Ardeth.

"Get up, lazy!" the latter ordered. "It's late! Your aunt has been up for at least half an hour."

"Jumping fishes!' Judy exclaimed in dismay. dragging herself from beneath the covers. "I must have slept like a log all night."

"I know I did,' Ardeth confessed. "What a fine pair of guards we proved to be!"

"Well, at least nothing went wrong here," Judy said, pulling on her shoes. "I'm relieved on that score."

Dressing fast, the girls hastened to the kitchen. Miss Meadows had the stove going and was cooking cereal. She appeared pale, however, and there were dark shadows under her eyes.

"Did you sleep well, Aunt Mattie?" Judy asked politely.

"Very badly."

Judy and Ardeth exchanged a quick, worried glance. Both hesitated to ask the question which was foremost in their minds.

"Did—did anything disturb you?" Judy managed finally.

"I never sleep well the first night in a strange place. I was awake for hours."

Judy drew a long breath and grinned at Ardeth. But her relief was brief. For Aunt Mattie went on impressively:

"I'm not sure I'll like this place as well as I thought last night. There's entirely too much traffic on the side road."

"You mean the main road, don't you, Aunt Mattie?" Judy corrected.

Miss Meadows stirred the pot of cereal on the stove. "I mean that highway that runs down the hill toward the river."

"Why, that's a private road and it dead-ends," Judy responded. "There's never any traffic in that direction."

"There was last night," Miss Meadows insisted firmly. "A truck came along the highway and stopped so that the headbeams shone almost directly into my window. The driver flashed them on and off several times as if in signal. Then, the lights were doused, and the truck turned down the side road."

"I can't imagine a truck using that road at night," Judy said thoughtfully. "The road doesn't go anywhere except to the cave. Perhaps you were mistaken, Aunt Mattie. Don't you think the truck might have gone on down the main highway?"

"I don't think so," Miss Meadows replied. "No, I'm sure the truck turned down the side road."

No more was said about the matter then. But after the breakfast dishes had been done, Ardeth and Judy slipped outside for a private talk.

"Do you suppose your aunt was right about those truck lights?" Ardeth asked, lowering her voice so it would not carry through the open kitchen window. "And what about that signal?"

"She must have been mistaken," Judy replied anxiously. "All the same, we certainly should investigate. Come on, Ardeth! If that truck turned down the dead-end road, there will be tire marks to prove it."

Chapter 13

THE MISSING KEY

CUTTING across the lawn which was heavy with dew, the two girls turned toward the entrance to the private road. A haze of smoke still hung above the treetops, but it was evident that the fire which had alarmed everyone the previous day, now was well under control.

Suddenly, Judy halted, staring at tire marks on the dirt road.

"Aunt Mattie was right!" she exclaimed. "A big truck did turn off the main highway!"

"The tire prints are plain to see," Ardeth agreed, equally startled. "But what would a heavy truck be doing here? The road dead-ends."

"It seems odd."

"Perhaps the driver only pulled off the pavement to fix a tire."

Judy shook her head. "The tracks plainly go down the slope toward the cave," she pointed out.

"Mightn't it have been a forest ranger fire fighting truck?"

"That's so," Judy acknowledged, "it might have been. Maybe that would explain the headlight signals Aunt Mattie reported seeing. I can't imagine though, why a Forest Service truck would use this road at night. The fire was across the river."

As the girls considered whether to go farther down the private road, they heard the rattle of a milk wagon approaching on the main highway.

"It's Bart!" Judy cried.

The delivery truck stopped some distance away, but after milk had been left at Calico Cottage, came on down the road. Bart drew up to chat with the girls.

"How's everything?" he inquired cheerfully. "Your ghost behaving himself?"

Judy replied that the household had not been disturbed further by the mysterious flute player. She added, however, that her aunt had slept badly and that lights from a truck had bothered her.

"I guess it must have been a Forest Service truck that went down this road last night," Ardeth remarked. "See the tire tracks."

Bart already had stepped out of the milk wagon to inspect them.

"Those weren't made by a Forest Service truck," he told the girls. "Their vehicles are lighter. Anyway, I don't know what a forest truck would be doing here late at night. Seems sort of queer—"

"I thought so myself!" Judy said quickly.

"Let's have a look-see," Bart proposed. "Want to ride down the hill with me? If you do, hop in!"

Judy and Ardeth scrambled into the cab, taking care not to step on Pete who was asleep on the floor.

"Do you dare leave your milk route?" Ardeth asked the young driver.

"I'm ahead of schedule this morning," Bart answered. "I can take a few minutes. This is my last week on the route anyway."

"You're taking another job?" Ardeth inquired politely.

By this time the milk truck had turned and was moving slowly down the narrow, rutty road.

"Not exactly," Bart admitted. "I've saved enough money to see me through a year of college. I'm laying off because I want to do a little exploring before I start in at school this fall."

"Exploring?" Judy repeated with interest. "Of the cavern?"

"That's right." Bart grinned, as he slowed down for a bad hole in the road. "Folks hereabouts think I'm crazy to spend so much time in a cave. It's in my blood, I guess! I'm planning on becoming a scientist if I make the grade."

"Does Calico Cave have any bats or other interesting birds or animals?" Ardeth questioned abruptly.

"Hundreds of bats. You can see them clustered in masses on the walls in one section of the cave, near the entrance."

"Ugh!" Judy shuddered.

"Why, they're harmless," Bart assured her. "I suppose you think of a bat as a naked, winged creature with claws that would catch in your hair?"

"I never came very close to one," Judy admitted, "but I do feel that way about them."

"Like a great many folks, you do the bat an injustice," Bart returned. "It's little claws are used only to provide a means of clinging to a rock wall. Bats are afraid of people. They fly at amazing speed, but they can dodge any obstacle."

"They sleep in the caves?" Ardeth questioned.

"Yes, the bat, you know, is descended from an animal that lived in a warm, uniform climate. For some reason, the bat never has been able to adapt itself to weather changes, so it hibernates in caves which have an almost constant temperature."

"I'd give anything if I had a bat!" Ardeth announced. "Just one!"

"A bat? What would you want with it?" Bart asked, rather amused by the remark.

Ardeth told him about the nature treasure chest at Pine Cone Camp. "Our unit hasn't contributed anything, as yet," she added. "If I could get one of those bats, we'd really be the talk of the camp."

"I think I can get you one," Bart offered, glancing at his wristwatch. "You're serious about wanting it?"

"Oh, yes, but I don't want to delay you on your run."

"If the bats are where I think they'll be, I can pick one off the wall in a minute or two," Bart promised. "Want to go into the cave with me?"

"I don't think we should without permission from our leader," Judy said quickly.

"I can travel faster alone at any rate," the young milkman replied.

As the milk truck rattled on down the winding road, he talked enthusiastically about bats and their habits.

The creatures, he told the girls, had silky, translucent wings and flew with astonishing precision.

"I've seen 'em fly between water and ceiling down deep in the cave where there was barely clearance," he related. "Now, if only I were a bat, I'd explore that siphon!"

"You shouldn't even think of such a thing!" Judy chided. "It would be frightfully dangerous."

Bart made no answer.

"You're not considering it, are you?" Judy demanded, alarmed by his silence.

"I've considered it for years," Bart answered soberly. "I think about it all the time, in fact. I've just about decided—" he deliberately broke off, and finished: "Now to tell you more about bats—they hang to the ceilings by their feet, head down. Their bodies are covered by their long, folded wings when they sleep. One can pick them off the wall, and they make no fuss."

"Ardeth, must you have a bat?" Judy tried to discourage her.

"Oh, yes, if I can get one without causing too much trouble. But how will I get it to camp?"

Bart had pulled up at the end of the private road. From the back end of the truck, he brought out a cardboard box with a cover.

"We can use this," he suggested. "I may not get a bat for you though. I haven't long to ramble through the cave this trip."

Tucking the cardboard box under his arm, the cheerful young milkman stepped from the truck. Alertly he gazed at a sizeable slick of oil on the roadside, remarking that it evidently had leaked from the parked truck.

"Apparently, it stayed here quite a while last night before turning around and pulling out," he added.

"What would a truck be doing down here late at night?" Judy speculated.

"I wouldn't know," Bart answered with a shrug. "Interesting question though."

He started off down the path which led to Calico Cave. Before vanishing from view amid the bushes, he paused to fling over his shoulder: "Don't try to follow me, even if I'm not back in a few minutes. Wait in the milk wagon."

Ten minutes elapsed, then fifteen and twenty. Eagerly the girls began to watch the path for their friend to reappear.

The rising sun beat down harder and harder on the milk wagon, causing Judy and Ardeth increasing discomfort. They became restless.

"It's taking Bart an awfully long time," Ardeth

remarked uneasily. "Perhaps I shouldn't have asked him to get a bat for me. If anything should happen—"

"He'll be along soon," Judy said. "I think I hear him coming now."

She was right, for a moment later, the young milkman emerged from the tunnel of branches at the trail's exit.

"Did you get one?" Ardeth cried eagerly.

"Sure did," Bart responded.

Coming over to the milk truck, he opened the punctured lid of the cardboard box, so that the girls could peep at the frightened creature flopping inside.

"After you've displayed him at camp, better let him fly away," the milkman advised. "He'll find his way back to the cave."

"Oh, I wouldn't want to keep him shut up," Ardeth replied. "That would be cruel. I promise to let him go by tonight."

"Fine!" Bart approved, climbing into the milk wagon and starting the motor. "Now I want you girls to make me another one."

"Another promise?" asked Ardeth, carefully holding the box Bart had placed in her hands.

"Yes, I want you to stay away from here unless you're with a forest ranger or some man."

"Away from the cave, you mean?" Judy questioned, rather surprised by the request.

"From the cave, and also away from this private road."

"But why?"

"I'll tell you," Bart said soberly. By this time he had turned the milk truck around in the narrow road and had headed it up the hill. "There's something going on here that will bear investigation."

"The truck tire tracks, you mean?" interposed Ardeth, mystified by the remark.

"At first, that didn't seem very disturbing," Bart said. "But I've since made a discovery. That was why it took me so long."

"You didn't run into anyone in the cave?" Judy asked quickly.

"No, but someone has been there recently. Last night probably."

"How do you know?"

"Someone had trampled the path to the cave. Boot tracks. Then inside the entrance chamber, I found cigarette butts and long marks, showing where heavy objects had been dragged across the floor. Boxes, I'd judge."

"All removed?" Judy questioned.

"Yes, no sign of anyone or anything in the cave now."

"You think someone must have come here last night in that truck and used the cave?"

"Obviously, Judy. But don't quiz me, because I've told you everything I learned. I'm not venturing any guesses as to who it was or why the person or persons came here late at night. My advice is just to keep clear of the place until we can learn what's going on."

"Judy and I are returning to camp this morning," Ardeth informed the young milkman. "So even if we wanted to prowl around, we wouldn't have an opportunity."

"That's all to the good then," Bart grinned. "There may be no cause for alarm, but it's just as well not to take chances."

At the turn-off onto the paved road, he said goodbye to the Scouts and resumed his milk route.

Triumphantly, Ardeth and Judy bore their captured bat to Calico Cottage where they displayed it to Miss Meadows. Though they related how they had obtained the creature, they did not repeat Bart's warning or mention what they had learned about the big truck.

Miss Meadow seemed to have forgotten the disturbance of the previous night completely. After making a show of admiring the imprisoned bat, she chirped:

"While you girls were away, I cleaned the cupboards."

"They're very neat and tidy now," Judy said, opening the double doors to inspect the rows of China.

"At the back of the cupboard, I found a key," Miss Meadows remarked casually. She produced it from her apron pocket. "Apparently, it fits a door. But which one I wouldn't know."

Judy rocked back on her heels and looked quickly at Ardeth. Neither spoke for a moment.

Finally, Judy trusted her voice. Taking care to keep it steady, to give no hint of her excitment and hope, she said quietly:

"I wouldn't be surprised if that key fits the cellar door, Aunt Mattie."

"Why, it might at that."

Judy forced herself to speak casually, as if the matter were of no great moment.

"The key looks about the right size," she remarked. "Do you mind if I try it?"

Chapter 14

A FAMILIAR FACE

MISS Meadows willingly relinquished the key which she had found in the kitchen cupboard.

Judy fitted it in the door lock and was elated when it turned readily. Her pose of indifference instantly dissolved.

"Now we can get into the cellar!" she exulted. "Whoopee!"

Miss Meadows could not understand her niece's exuberance. The key was only an ordinary one so far as she knew, and until that moment she scarcely had noted that the basement was closed off.

The opening of the cellar door had brought a whiff of stale, cool air into the kitchen.

Poised at the head of the long flight of stone stairs, Judy peered down into the darkness. In vain she groped for a light switch.

"I guess the cellar never was equipped with electricity," she remarked. "I'll get my flashlight."

She ran to the bedroom, returning a moment later to find Miss Meadows regarding the stairway with disapproval.

"Need we go down there, Judy?" she asked to

discourage her. "Since the door was locked, the cottage owner might prefer us to keep it so."

"Oh, we can relock the door," Judy answered, flashing her light over the rough brick wall along the steep stairway. "First though, I want to see what's below."

Focusing her light upon the uneven stone steps, she cautiously started down.

"Watch your footing," she advised Ardeth and her aunt, who followed close behind. "These steps are narrow and worn."

Miss Meadows remarked that the cellar seemed very old in contrast to the new cottage.

"It is old," Judy agreed. "When Mr. Krumm built the cottage, he tried to save money by using the foundation of Captain Hager's place."

Judy negotiated the stairway safely and waited for the others at a jagged doorway which opened into the main cellar chamber.

The basement was very still, except for the shuffle of the descending feet.

"No musical chimes or the like?" Ardeth de-demanded with a suppressed giggle as she reached the bottom of the stairway.

Moving through the stone archway, the three found themselves in a large room. The chamber was dry, but nevertheless gave forth a musty odor.

The ancient brick walls were lined with shelves, all of which appeared empty. In fact, the only visible objects in the room were a half dozen old barrels. The casks lay helter-skelter, some on their sides, and other up-ended.

Judy deliberately walked around the barrels, inspecting them closely and kicking at them with her foot. All gave forth a hollow sound, which echoed in the chamber room.

Satisfied that every cask was empty, Judy next turned her attention to a smaller storage closet off to the left.

"This must have been the fruit and vegetable storage room," she declared. "It's been cleaned out though."

The shelves were completely bare, and the roving flashlight revealed only an undisturbed layer of dust.

"We've seen everything," Ardeth said, losing interest. "I think we should be getting upstairs. The camp station wagon will be coming for us any minute now."

It was well that they had cut short their inspection of the basement, for within five minutes the camp station wagon drove up.

In a flurry to be off, Judy and Ardeth hurriedly gathered their few belongings and the precious bat from Calico Cave.

"Now have a good time in camp and don't keep trying to look after me," Miss Meadows admonished as she bade the girls goodbye. "Drop by whenever you feel like it, but don't think you have to stay here over night."

"I don't like you to remain alone," Judy began only to have her aunt interrupt.

"Nonsense! I'll be all right. Now run along, and enjoy your friends."

In truth, Judy was somewhat relieved to know that there was no reason for the Scouts to remain each night at Calico Cottage. Although the mysterious flute sounds had not been explained, and might never be, she and Ardeth had convinced themselves that no danger lurked in the cellar.

As for Bart's warning not to go near the cave without a male escort, Judy decided that to pass on the admonition to her aunt, might only cause uneasiness.

"Aunt Mattie never will set foot inside that cave," she reflected. "So why worry her needlessly? She'll probably never see those truck lights again."

At Pine Cone Camp a few minutes later, Judy and Ardeth created a sensation by producing their captive bat. The other Scouts generously credited the Beaver Patrol girls with having the very best treasure chest entry. Everyone was satified when Miss Lubell announced that they had won the competition.

"We certainly got in just under the wire," Ardeth chuckled, when informed that her bat had taken first honors. "Now I'll let him fly away, and hope he returns to Calico Cave safely."

Making up for time which of necessity had been spent away from camp, Judy had a wonderful day with her friends. She swam, went sailboating, and in the late afternoon helped set the table for the evening meal.

Later that night, all the girls enjoyed a sing-fest and took part in folk dancing.

"What a grand day!" Judy declared blissfully as she sought her tent a few minutes before the "lights out" signal. "I hope Aunt Mattie doesn't run into trouble. I feel guilty, knowing she's alone at the cottage."

She dropped off to sleep quickly, determined to check on affairs at Calico Cottage the first thing in the morning.

Judy's intentions were the very best. Nevertheless, she awoke late and was hard pressed to dress and be on time for breakfast. Thereafter, she found herself assigned to kitchen detail with Beverly and Kathleen.

The three spent until lunch time peeling apples for pie and washing vegetables. Even after luncheon, Judy did not get to a telephone, for the unit leader hurried her off to her tent to prepare for a hike.

In connection with the hike, the Scouts planned to visit one of the nearby ranger towers. A brisk walk through the forest, brought them presently to a cleared area from which arose a tall, steel framework.

The Scouts climbed the steep stairway to a glassed-in square observation room. A ranger, who had been poring over a map on a table, greeted the visitors in a friendly way and invited them to look about.

After answering a number of questions, he showed the girls an automatic fire-finder, an instrument which permitted an observer to read with precision both vertical and horizontal angles. By means of the device, a newly discovered fire could be pinpointed and rangers immediately dispatched to the area.

"We have a network of ten observation towers in this particular area," he informed the Scouts. "Even so all points cannot be viewed, so we find it necessary to maintain ground patrols as well."

"Can one see Pine Cone Camp from here?" Judy inquired.

"No, the camp is one of our blind spots, unfortunately," the ranger replied. "Rest assured, it is well protected though. Lowell Diethelm patrols that area. His Forest Service car is equipped with radio telephone. If he should observe a fire, he immediately would notify headquarters. Ground fighters would be dispatched at once."

"Do you have many fires here during the summers?" Kathleen inquired.

"Until this year, very few. Recently, we've had a number of small ones, mostly along the main highway. A few though, have been of mysterious origin."

"Deliberately set?" questioned Judy.

"We're beginning to wonder," the ranger answered. "Carelessness, of course, is the underlying cause of most fires. But incendiarism runs high too. Now that so many summer campers and tourists are pouring into the area, we have to be especially watchful."

Before leaving the observation tower, the Scouts studied the big topographical map and took turns peering through the binoculars.

"Well, come again girls," the ranger invited as they prepared to leave. "Be careful of your fires. And remember, if you do see one, report it at once. Discovery time counts for a lot."

Leaving the observation tower, the Scouts hiked on for another mile and a half. By the time they reached the Fountain Falls trail, everyone was beginning to feel the first pangs of hunger.

"When do we eat?" Virginia demanded.

"Soon," promised the unit leader. "I'll get the fire started while you girls see the falls. I obtained a permit, so we're violating no rules to build our own."

The girls helped gather wood. Then, while the fire was burning down to bright cherry coals, those not delegated to watch, climbed a steep path to Foutain Falls.

A veil-like spray of water fell nearly thirty feet to a rocky shelf below. Ferns and moss protruded from cracks in the limestone rock.

After admiring the sight for some minutes, the

Scouts retraced their way to help with supper. Already a huge tin can was warming on the coals, filled with a fragrant chowder mixture of bacon, onions, canned corn and potatoes.

By the time Judy had toasted bread, the other simple items of the meal were ready. The crisp mountain air had given everyone enormous appetites. However, there was sufficient food for everyone.

Once the litter had been cleared away and the last marshmallow toasted, the unit leader personally supervised putting out the camp fire.

She had the girls smother it with water brought from the nearby creek. Then to make certain that not a spark remained, she covered the dead coals with a heavy layer of soil.

"Now it's time to hike down to Siverton," she advised the group as she consulted her watch. "The time has gone very fast."

The downhill hike was comparatively easy and the group made faster time than had been expected. As a consequence, they arrived in the village at twenty minutes to seven.

"We'll have a short wait until the station wagon comes," the unit leader told the girls. "It shouldn't be long though."

The group had been instructed to meet their driver at Luke's Cafe, one of the few business establishments open after six o'clock.

Accordingly, they went in, taking tables and

booths. Some of the girls ordered ice cream. Judy finished hers quickly, and then left the booth to pay her bill at the counter.

Two men were seated on stools, drinking coffee and munching hamburger sandwiches.

Judy cast an indifferent glance in their direction, and than looked again, more intently. One of the men she had never seen before, but she was certain she recognized the other.

"That's Joe Pompilli!" she thought excitedly. "The man who was hurt in the truck accident! The same hi-jacker that the State Highway Patrol wants to nail!"

As she considered what she should do, Kathleen sauntered out of another booth. Judy signaled to her.

Once Kathleen had joined her, she informed her of her suspicion.

Kathleen studied the man that Judy pointed out. "Yes, he's the one we helped!" she whispered. "The one who was called Joe!"

"He's wanted by the Highway Patrol," Judy replied grimly, her mind made up. "Kathleen, stay here and keep your eye on those two men. Don't let them recognize you, if you can prevent it. I'm going to slip out of here and telephone!"

Chapter 15

JUDY'S MISTAKE

RUSHING out of the cafe, Judy scarcely knew which way to go. Across the street, lights were on at the corner drugstore, so she decided to seek a telephone there.

As she darted to the opposite curb, she spied one of the forest rangers, who only that moment had emerged from a barber shop.

Judy had seen the Forest Service man several times since her arrival at Pine Cone Camp and knew that his name was Lowell Diethelm.

Now, instantly recognizing his face and uniform, a wave of relief swept over her. He would know how to help her notify the State Highway Patrol quickly!

"Oh, ranger!" she called, for in the excitement of the moment, his name temporarily fled from her mind.

"Yes?" The ranger turned to regard Judy with intent curiosity.

"Can you help me make a report to the State Highway Department right away?"

"Why sure," the ranger replied. "What's wrong? An automobile accident?"

Judy jerked her head to indicate the cafe across the street. "Two men are in there eating lunch," she explained, trying to hold her voice steady. "I'm sure one of them is Joe Pompilli!"

"Not the hi-jacker?"

Judy's head bobbed excitedly. "I know he's the same one Kathleen and I helped the other day when a truck went off the road. I want to get word to the State Highway Department right away."

"Take it easy," the ranger advised as Judy turned as if to start off alone. "You're mistaken, I think. Joe Pompili wouldn't dare to show himself openly here."

"It does seem a reckless thing for him to do," Judy conceded. "But I'm sure the man is the same one."

"You must be wrong, but to prove it I'll go over with you to the cafe," Diethelm offered.

Crossing the street, Judy and the ranger peered in through the big plate glass window. The two truckers still were seated at the lunch counter.

"Which one do you say is Joe?" the ranger demanded.

"The one with the square jaw, seated next to the wall. I never saw the other man before."

Diethelm began to chuckle in a hard sort of manner which grated unpleasantly on Judy's ears.

"Why are you laughing?" she asked. "Isn't that man Joe Pompilli?"

"Not on your life. Both those men are truckers

for the Peoria Cartage Co., and they make this town every few days. It's lucky you ran into me before you went blabbering your suspicions to the State Highway patrol. If you'd accused those two of being hi-jackers, they might not have liked it."

"But I can't understand it, unless I was misinformed by the state highwaymen," Judy stammered, completely crushed by the mistake she had made. "That man certainly was hurt in an accident. He's wearing a wrist bandage and there are cuts on his face! The other Scouts and myself gave him first aid treatment."

"I don't know about that," Ranger Diethelm replied with a shrug. "The state patrolmen either made a mistake in identifying him, or gave you the wrong dope."

"Shouldn't I call Highway headquarters to make sure?"

"You'll be making a silly mistake if you do," warned the ranger. "A mistake that will make your Scout organization the laughing stock of the community. Take my word for it, those two men are Jim Brady and Donald Fine, two highly respected truckers. But go ahead if you want to make the call."

Lowell Diethelm's words, and particularly his air of amusement, robbed Judy of all desire to risk action which might hold up her organization to possible ridicule.

JUDY'S MISTAKE

She hesitated. The ranger mistook her silence for unwillingness to follow his suggestion.

"Instead of trying to track down criminals, you Scouts would do better to look after affairs around your own camp," he said cuttingly.

"Why, what do you mean?" asked Judy, startled. She had detected a hostile note in the ranger's voice.

"You girls should be more careful about starting camp fires."

"We're always careful," Judy insisted indignantly.

"Didn't you have a fire this afternoon at Fountain Falls?"

"Yes, but we were granted a permit. We took great care with our fire, dousing the coals with water and covering the dead ashes with dirt as an added precaution."

"Well, not thirty minutes ago, our spotter at Tower 32 reported a small fire close to the Falls. Fortunately, it was put out before it spread."

"It couldn't have been our fire, and we shouldn't be blamed for it," Judy said, her eyes flashing.

"Some member of your party may have dropped a lighted match."

"None of us had any. Only our leader carried matches."

"Well, I don't know how the fire started," the ranger admitted. "Just be more careful, that's all. Now about reporting this trucker you think is Joe Pompilli—"

"I guess I must have made a mistake," Judy mumbled. "Sorry to have bothered you."

"No trouble at all," Diethelm replied, as he smiled as if suddenly relieved. "We rangers always try to be of service. Watch those fires now!"

Tipping his broad-brimmed hat, he sauntered on down the darkening street.

With mingled feelings, Judy was watching the retreating figure. Humiliated that she had made a mistake in identifying Joe Pompilli, she nevertheless was annoyed at the ranger for trying to accuse the Scouts in connection with a newly discovered fire."

"I think he dragged that in just to bother me," she thought resentfully. "But why should he take such an attitude?"

As Judy stood by the cafe window, wondering what to do, Kathleen signaled to her from the inside. Her friend's meaning was not immediately clear. Then she comprehended that the two truckers were paying their bill, preparatory to leaving the cafe.

"I'll have to let them go," Judy decided. "Nothing else to do."

A moment later the two truckers came outside. Judy did not try to stop them, but they passed almost in front of her.

The one she had taken to be Joe Pompille gazed squarely at her. Involuntarily, he half stopped.

JUDY'S MISTAKE

Then, deliberately turning his gaze away, he went on.

"He recognized me!" Judy thought, her pulse pounding. "I know he was that same man Kathleen and I helped on the road. He was called Joe too!"

Ignoring the girl entirely, the two men went on. Judy saw them get into a truck which bore the Peoria Cartage Co., name on its side. A moment before they drove away, she jotted down the license number.

She had just finished scribbling the numbers on the back of an old envelope, when Kathleen joined her.

"What happened?" her friend demanded. "I thought you were going to have those men arrested. Couldn't you reach the Highway Patrol station?"

"I didn't try," Judy confessed ruefully.

"You didnt try? Why not?"

Judy recounted her conversation with the ranger.

"He talked me out of it," she concluded. "I can't help thinking I made a mistake too. I wish I'd ignored his advice. It's too late now, of course."

"I know that man was the same one we met," Kathleen insisted.

"I'm sure of it too," Judy nodded. "Ranger Diethelm insists he's an ordinary trucker and his name is either Jim Brady or Donald Fine."

"Well, that doesn't fit in with what we learned," Kathleen declared, shaking her head. "That man was called Joe by his friend."

"I know," Judy agreed with a deep sigh. "I'm all mixed up. I guess the best thing to do is to forget those hi-jackers and let the state patrol handle the situation. I've made a mess of it!"

"No such thing," Kathleen insisted loyally. "We may have made a mistake, but if so, it wasn't our fault. We must have acted on mis-information."

Judy grinned and squeezed her friend's hand. "You're a dear," she said, "always bucking up my morale. Do me a favor?"

"Of course."

"Then, let's keep this little episode to ourselves. The other Scouts didn't hear about it?"

"No, I didn't say a word to anyone. I just kept out of view and watched those two men as you suggested."

"Good!" Judy drew a relieved sign. "If this gets out on me, my name will be mud! You know, I'm already being teased at Pine Cone Camp because of the Calico Cottage ghost!"

"We're all taking a ribbing because of that boy with the flute," Kathleen admitted. "Any theory as to what causes the strange sounds?"

"No, not yet," Judy replied. "Everything was quiet the last night I spent at the cottage. I'm wondering though, how Aunt Mattie got along last evening."

"Perhaps our driver will stop at the cottage for a few minutes, so we can check."

"I intend to ask him," Judy returned. "It must be seven o'clock now."

"It is, Kathleen agreed, "and our driver is coming now!"

She had sighted the familiar camp station wagon rounding a corner. It waited for a traffic light and then came on, to park in front of the restaurant.

The driver had been instructed to make two trips, as not all of the girls could be seated in the vehicle. Accordingly, he designated those who should remain behind.

Judy, Kathleen and other members of the Beaver Patrol, managed to find a place for themselves in the first load.

On short time, the driver told Judy he could not possibly wait at Calico Cottage. However, he compromised by agreeing to let her and Kathleen off there, while he continued on to camp. Then on the second trip, he would pick them up.

"Fine and dandy!" Judy approved. "That will give us nearly an hour to talk to Aunt Mattie and make certain everything is all right."

The station wagon climbed the darkening mountain road, presently halting near the cottage. As Kathleen and Judy alighted, they noticed that lights blazed everywhere inside the dwelling.

"Aunt Mattie is here all right!" Judy remarked, leading the way across the lawn. "I wonder why she has all the lights burning?"

"So early too," Kathleen added.

Even before the Scouts reached the front door, it was flung open by Miss Meadows, who had noted the arrival of the station wagon.

"Oh, I'm so glad you came!" the woman exclaimed.

Her face seemed drained of all color, and her eyes had a frightened look.

"Why, Aunt Mattie!" Judy exclaimed. "Is anything wrong?"

"This dreadful cottage!"

"You've been hearing music?" Judy surmized.

"Music?"

"What was it that upset you?" Judy asked, realizing she had made a poor guess. "Not another one of those mysterious telephone calls?"

"No! No!" Miss Meadows stepped back so that the girls might enter the cottage. "Just come in," she invited. "Then you'll hear for yourselves, and I won't need to explain!"

Chapter 16

ANOTHER DISTURBANCE

SCARCELY knowing what to expect, Judy and Kathleen entered Calico Cottage. Everything appeared quite normal, except that a chair in the kitchen had been overturned.

"I upset it myself," Miss Meadows explained. "I —I was rather excited, I'm afraid."

"Tell us what happened, Aunt Mattie," Judy urged. "What disturbed you?"

"It was a dreadful sound from the basement. A sort of moan as if someone were in pain. And then to top it, there came a series of loud thumps, very much like muffled thunder."

"That couldn't have been someone setting off dynamite at a distance?" Kathleen suggested. "I know the rangers were blasting trees in the park area."

"This sound came from the cellar," Miss Meadows insisted.

"How long ago, Aunt Mattie?" questioned Judy.

"About ten minutes, I'd judge."

"Did you go down there to check?"

"To the cellar?" Miss Meadows demanded. "I most assuredly did not!"

"Then I guess the job is up to us," Judy said, looking directly at Kathleen. "Where's that key?"

"I don't think you should go down into that dreary hole," Miss Meadows protested.

"Nonsense, Aunt Mattie! We investigated once before, and everything was all right. You've not had the door unlocked since?"

"Absolutely, not. I've been here at the cottage all the while too."

"Then no one could be down there."

"I didn't imagine those weird sounds," Miss Meadows said. "If you had been here—"

Suddenly she stiffened. From beneath the kitchen floor there issued forth a series of muffled thuds.

"Hear it?" Miss Meadows whispered, staring fixedly at the locked cellar door.

The sound ceased and the cottage was as quiet as before. Judy and Kathleen stood transfixed, dreading to take the action which they felt they must.

"Where's that key?" Judy finally murmured, groping for it on the high kitchen shelf.

"Don't go down there," Miss Meadows advised nervously. "It might be dangerous."

"It's worse not to investigate," Judy insisted. "You can't stay here and live in constant dread."

Her fingers closed upon the key. She unlocked the door, but hesitated as she peered down the dark stairway.

ANOTHER DISTURBANCE

"Do you have a flashlight?" she asked Kathleen, who huddled at her elbow.

"In my knapsack," Kathleen replied. "But I left it on the station wagon, never thinking I'd want it here."

"There are candles on the shelf," Miss Meadows remembered. "I'll get one, if you insist on going down there. I'd rather just move out of this place though!"

"I don't know where you'll find another cottage on short notice," Judy told her regretfully. "Everything around here has been taken."

"I can go to a hotel."

"The closest one is eighteen miles away. Aunt Mattie, I don't like to urge you to stay, but there must be a logical explanation for these strange noises. I mean to find it too! Let me have one of those candles."

Miss Meadows found it for her, and lighted the wick.

"Watch the drip of the wax," she advised, "or you'll burn your hand."

The glowing candle made a flickering, ghostly circle of light on rough walls of the stairway.

Resolutely, Judy started down. Close behind her came Kathleen, while Miss Meadows unwillingly brought up the rear.

Judy descended a half dozen steps, only to pause. A slight breath of air, caused the candle to waver and nearly go out. And at the same moment, she caught an unpleasant odor which seemed to rise from the darkness below.

"Mercy!" gasped Miss Meadows, as she too sniffed the air.

The musty scent became stronger as the three went on down. Judy localized it in the main cellar room, toward the south east wall.

However, in slowly moving the candle about, she could find no cause for the unpleasant odor.

"It's such a strange smell," Kathleen commented with a nervous shiver. "A sort of stale air scent. But from where does it come?"

Judy asked Kathleen to hold the candle. Carefully, she ran her hand over the brick wall, feeling along the line of crumbling mortar.

"There's an opening here!" she suddenly exclaimed. "I can feel cool air coming in!"

Excited by Judy's discovery, Kathleen held the candle higher.

As she raised it in line with the brick which Judy's exploring hand had found, a direct current of air extinguished the flame.

The three were left in total darkness.

"I'll get some matches," Miss Meadows said eager to be out of the basement. "But is there any need to explore further? Haven't we discovered everything there is to learn?"

"Not quite everything," said Judy. "We've learned

ANOTHER DISTURBANCE

where that musty odor comes from though. It is being blasted in through the broken mortar."

"How strange," Kathleen murmured. "Shouldn't there be solid dirt or rock behind these walls and under the floor?"

"One would think so," Judy agreed thoughtfully, "unless—"

"There might be a tunnel connected with the cottage!" Kathleen speculated.

"A tunnel, possibly tied up with Calico Cave," Judy carried on the thought. "Even so, that doesn't explain those strange banging noises."

Leaving the girls alone in the cellar, Miss Meadows went quickly for matches. She returned promptly and the candle was religthed.

This time, Judy was careful to shield it with her hand so that it would not be blown out.

In the uncertain light, the three were able to see a faint, rectangular outline on the wall, which marked a division between old and newer bricks.

"At one time, there must have been an opening here!" Judy asserted, elated by her disccovery. "A long while ago, apparently, the passageway or whatever it is, was bricked over. Now that the mortar is falling away, cold air filters in."

"From where?" Kathleen demanded.

"That's what we'll have to learn, if we can. I have a hunch Captain Hager might be able to supply interesting information."

"I'll bet he could at that!" cried Kathleen. "Since he lived in the old house so many years, he must have known about this bricked up place on the wall. In fact, he may have closed it himself."

"The captain hinted that Mr. Krumm made a bad mistake in building the cottage on the old foundation," Judy recalled. "I'm sure he knows a lot about this place that he hasn't told!"

"Say, wouldn't it be great if we could solve the mystery before we leave Pine Cone Camp? You'd win a rental bonus too from Mr. Krumm, Judy!"

"I don't care about that part, but it would be fun to hit upon an explanation for everything that's happened here. The thing that puzzles me most is that boy with the flute—"

"Boy with a flute?" Miss Meadow interposed, her voice rising.

Judy regretted her slip of tongue. Nevertheless, having made the mistake, she could do no less than tell her aunt about the strange musical notes which had startled the Scouts during the night they had spent at the cottage.

"What manner of place have I rented?" Miss Meadows gasped. "Is the cottage haunted?"

"By the spirit of the White Witch," Judy said with a giggle. Then, becoming sober, she added: "I'm sure there's no danger here, Aunt Mattie. Even so, you mustn't stay another night. Come with us to Pine Cone Camp. We'll find a bed for you, and tomorrow we can start looking for another cottage."

"And have everyone say I was frightened away?" Miss Meadows reproved her niece. "The very idea!"

"You mean you're willing to stay?"

"Yes, I intend to," Miss Meadows announced firmly. "At least for a day or so."

"I'll remain with you," Judy offered. "Not that I'll be any protection."

To her surprise, Miss Meadows turned her aside. "No," she told Judy, "you've already lost a great deal of camp fun on my account. You're not to worry about me any more, or Calico Cottage."

"But to leave you alone—"

"I'll manage," Miss Meadows said dryly. "Let's go upstairs now, or you girls will miss your station wagon."

"Goodness, I forgot about the driver calling for us!" Kathleen exclaimed. "We've been down here in the cellar quite a while."

Hastily, the three ascended to the main floor of the cottage. Miss Meadows locked the cellar door and replaced the key on the cupboard shelf.

"I intend to forget about those stupid noises," she asserted. "It will take a very powerful ghost indeed to dislodge me from my bed tonight."

Greatly relieved that her aunt was taking such a matter-of-fact view of an unpleasant situation, Judy said no more about the disturbances. She and Kathleen began to watch for the camp station wagon, and ten minutes later, saw its headlights wink in signal from the main road.

"Goodbye, Aunt Mattie," Judy said, giving her a hasty peck on the cheek. "If anything should go wrong tonight, you'll call me at Pine Cone Camp?"

"I'll call the police," Miss Meadows threatened. "Now run along, and enjoy yourselves."

Enroute back to camp, Judy and Kathleen did not report their experience at Calico Cottage. During the drive up the mountain, they were somewhat silent, but the others took it for granted that the two girls were worn out from the day's hike.

In truth, Judy was very tired. Even before the "lights out" signal, she was snug in her cot, with the warm blankets tucked around her ears.

"I feel as if I could sleep until noon tomorrow," she murmured drowsily. "Is there any law, I wonder, about skipping breakfast, and staying in bed?"

If there was an answer to her question, Judy did not hear it. She fell into a sound slumber, lulled by the chirp of crickets.

Sometime toward morning, Judy began to dream. A confusion of images flitted through her mind. She thought she was exploring a cave, that the White Witch had come alive and was advancing toward her in a menacing manner.

In her dream, she became aware of a horrible odor. The scent enveloped her, stifling her so that she could not breathe.

Awakening, Judy found herself battling the blankets which she had pulled up over her head. She laughed in relief. The White Witch was only a

ANOTHER DISTURBANCE 149

nightmare! There was no disagreeable odor—or was there?

Thrusting the covers aside, Judy sat up in bed. Fearfully, she sniffed the air. The odor had not been entirely in her dream! The air was chilly, filled with an acrid scent she could not identify immediately.

Then suddenly, Judy knew. She bolted out of bed, the cold chills racing down her spine. The tent was filled with smoke! The camp must be afire!

Chapter 17

SMOKE IN THE WOODS

THOROUGHLY alert now, Judy awakened her tent mates, warning them of the danger.

"What's this?" mumbled Ardeth, drugged by sleep and unwilling to leave her comfortable cot.

"Get out of here fast, unless you want to be burned!" Judy said tersely, giving her a hard shake. "The forest is on fire!"

The other Beaver Patrol Scouts who shared the tent, already were out of bed and dressing with frenzied haste. Judy pulled on her own clothes, aware that more and more smoke was swirling about the canvas shelter.

Once outside, she saw the source of the fire. Heavy black smoke was billowing toward the camp from the woods where duff and debris were ablaze.

Judy's first moment of relief that camp buildings and tents were intact, gave way to concern. The surface fire was dangerously close. Fed by a light but steady wind, the flames were moving toward the camp with amazing speed!

As she started for the adjoining tents to awaken the girls there, a gong in the main dining room sounded the first alarm.

SMOKE IN THE WOODS

Bong! Bong! Bong!

Tent flaps went apart, and sleep-eyed Scouts began to thrust touseled heads out into the cold night air.

"What's up?" demanded Beverly, one of the first Beaver Patrol girls to scramble into her clothes. "Is the camp afire?"

"Not yet, but it will be if we don't work fast!" Judy asserted. "Oh!"

She uttered a little scream as a flying brand, borne by the wind, dropped in the grass only a few feet away.

Badly frightened, she and Beverly ran to stamp out the tiny flames.

By this time, the camp was in confusion. Scouts were pouring out of their tents, milling about, chattering excitedly.

Unit leaders quickly gained control of the situation, ordering everyone to the main lodge assembly room.

Miss Lubell spoke tersely to the girls.

"Now there is no cause for alarm," she advised everyone. "The fire is very close to our camp, and the wind is in this direction, but rangers are on their way here. I notified them by telephone. The fire already had been spotted from the observation tower."

"Will we have to evacuate the camp?" inquired Miss Ward.

"That depends entirely upon whether or not the

fire can quickly be brought under control," the camp director replied. "So far, it is not wide-spread, but the head is moving in this direction."

"Can't we do anything until the rangers come?" Judy interposed.

"We can," Miss Lubell said. "We can't hope to fight the fire, but we can take steps to keep it under control. Each unit is to report to its leader and follow her orders. We'll wet down the tents and the buildings to protect them from flying sparks. Then we'll make a fire break by clearing a ditch ahead of the spreading flames!"

Pouring out of the assembly hall, the Beaver Patrol Scouts clustered about their unit leader and Miss Ward. Under direction, they carried buckets of water from the lake, dousing the walls of their tents thoroughly.

To be prepared for a quick evacuation, in the event one was ordered, they hastily tossed their belongings into suitcases.

This done, they raced to the edge of the camp, to assist counselors, who had frantically started to dig a shallow trench or fire break.

Using garden hoes, rakes, spades and other implements at hand, the Scouts rapidly cleared a band several feet wide between the camp and the spreading ground fire.

A few sparks were flying, but those which dropped in dry grass, were instantly extinguished by a unit assigned to that particular task.

SMOKE IN THE WOODS 153

By this time, the wind had spread the fire into an elliptical shape. Inexorably, it crept nearer and nearer the trench the girls were digging.

"It's going to be nip and tuck to save the camp," Miss Lubell gasped. "Don't give up, girls!"

Against the flames, trees were silhouetted as dark, towering shapes. The sight was a terrifying one. But even though they could feel the heat in their faces, the Scouts kept doggedly at work.

Then suddenly a cry went up.

"The rangers!" cried a Lone Tree Scout. "They've come!"

Judy drew a deep, tired sigh of relief as she saw the Forest Service truck roll in with fire-fighting equipment.

"Our job is done now," Miss Lubell said, wiping a smudge from her cheek. "We'll let the men take over. Everyone report in the assembly room."

The Scouts all checked in, and after washing up, watched the crew of rangers attack the fire.

A tractor widened and completed the ditch started by the Scouts. This task accomplished, rangers beat out some of the flames which had jumped the "break," and hooked up a power pump.

Sleep was out of the question for the excited Scouts. They kept in orderly groups, but remained at the assembly room windows, watching every phase of the efficient fire fighting work.

The Beaver Patrol girls, those of the Lone Tree unit, and the Oriole outfit, volunteered to help in the kitchen. Gallons of coffee were prepared for the rangers.

"We've made enough for an army of workers!" Judy laughed.

The beverage was kept hot, ready to serve whenever a tired fire fighter could leave his post.

By four o'clock, the rangers announced that the fire finally was under complete control. Relaxing a bit from their arduous labors, the men took turns dropping around at the kitchen for coffee and a sandwich.

Arthur Wentz, one of the first rangers to come, praised the Scouts warmly for their well organized efforts prior to the arrival of the forest service truck.

"This could have been a bad fire," he remarked. "There are three types—surface, ground and crown. But all start as surface fires."

Judy asked the ranger to distinguish between the different classifications.

"Surface fires, as the name implies, burn only the loose debris on top of the ground," he explained. "That's the type of thing we encountered here. Sometimes, the fire eats down into the layer of undecomposed material on the forest floor, and then you have a ground fire. The most difficult of all are those which spread into the trees, or the crown fires."

"How do you suppose this one started?" Miss Ward asked the ranger.

"That's hard to say," he replied.

Lowell Diethelm, the ranger Judy had met in the village the previous evening, now tramped into the kitchen. He had overheard Miss Ward's question and the reply.

"It's plain enough how the fire started," he commented, pouring himself a mug of coffee.

"How?" Judy asked.

"Someone from this camp has been careless about fire."

A stunned silence followed the observation. Then, almost as a unit, the Girl Scouts began to protest.

"I don't think that's fair to say!" exclaimed Kathleen indignantly. "Do you have any proof that the fire was started by anyone in this camp?"

"No proof," the ranger admitted. "Just circumstantial evidence. You girls had a cook-out last night?"

"We started a fire at Fountain Falls," Judy said. "You knew about that. We put it out too!"

"Anyway, that's miles from here!" Betty Bashe broke in. "This fire started close to our camp."

"Exactly my point," replied Diethelm. "Any other cook-outs last night?"

"Our unit had one," spoke up a Scout from the Lone Tree patrol. "We were accompanied by our leaders though, and built our fire on a rock. Every spark was extinguished before we left the spot."

"That's what you thought," Diethelm said, none too pleasantly. "I'm not saying the Scouts started this fire, but I do say, it looks rather suspicious. If the fire hadn't been reported so quickly, the entire camp might have burned."

"That's for sure," agreed Arthur Wentz. "But I think you're being unjust to the girls, Lowell. The fire may have been started by a carelessly dropped cigarette or a match. Or it could have been deliberately set."

"What's that?" Diethelm demanded, startled.

"Just a little thought I had," Wentz replied with an odd smile.

Diethelm seemed to have been made uncomfortable by the remark and pursued the subject no further. He gulped down his coffee and soon left the kitchen.

"Don't take what he said too seriously," Wentz told the Scouts. "This camp has a good record. No one knows how the fire started."

"I can assure you that it was not touched off by any of our girls," asserted Miss Lubell firmly. "We've taken every precaution against fire."

Although heavy smoke still hung over the camp area, the flames no longer were spreading. A ranger was assigned to remain behind to watch the smoldering debris. The others loaded their truck and presently drove away.

Worn out by their strenuous activities, the Scouts returned to their cots to try to snatch a few winks of sleep before dawn. Their eyes smarted, but tired as they were, they were too excited to relax. Most of the girls were relieved when the gong sounded as

SMOKE IN THE WOODS

a signal for them to dress again and assemble for breakfast.

Great quantities of hot chocolate, scrambled eggs, toast and fruit, brought cheer to the Scouts. Nevertheless, the main topic at the table was the unjust accusation which Lowell Diethelm had leveled at the organization.

"I've never liked that ranger," Judy remarked to Virginia, who sat beside her. "I guess it's mean to say, because a Girl Scout should try to like folks, but there's something about him—"

"I know what you mean," nodded Virginia, reaching for another piece of toast. "He doesn't seem friendly as the other rangers do."

"I can't get over what happened today about that trucker," Judy went on, thinking aloud. "Suppose I was right, and Diethelm was mistaken—"

She broke off then, for Miss Ward had come into the dining hall, and was signaling to her.

"Judy, you're wanted at the telephone," the teacher called. "Your aunt, I think."

Judy went quickly to Miss Lubell's office. The call must be important, she reasoned, else her aunt would not have phoned at such an early morning hour. She was afraid Aunt Mattie had learned of the fire and was alarmed for her safety. Either that, or the ghost of Calico Cottage had put in another appearance!

As she took down the receiver, her first fears were confirmed. Miss Meadows was in a great state of agitation, having been informed that a fire was raging at Pine Cone Camp.

"It was only a little fire, and it never reached our camp," Judy explained patiently. "Now don't worry one tiny bit, Aunt Mattie! Everything is all right here."

"Well, that's a relief," Miss Meadows sighed. "I confess, I've spent a dreadful night."

"No more disturbances, I hope."

"It depends upon what you mean by disturbances," Miss Meadows returned stiffly. "There were no weird sounds from the basement. But other things happened."

"What sort of things?"

"I can't tell you over the telephone," Miss Meadows answered. "Just come as quickly as you can to the cottage!"

And with that, she hung up the receiver.

Chapter 18

AN URGENT CALL

IT was well after seven o'clock when Judy, accompanied by Kathleen, arrived at Calico Cottage.

The trip down the mountain in the station wagon had not been without excitement. Less than a half mile from the cottage, the driver had been halted by state patrolmen, who had set up a road block.

At first, the girls had assumed that motorists on the main highway were being stopped because of the fire which still smoldered in the Pine Cone Camp area. Therefore, it came as a surprise to learn that the road block had been set up for an entirely different purpose.

The state highway patrolman informed them that a truckload of auto parts had been hi-jacked during the night on a lonely stretch of road between the towns of Silverton and Grove City, some miles away. The truck was known to have followed the mountain road, making for the state line, yet had seemed to disappear into thin air.

"Somehow those birds get wind of where our road blocks are set up," the highway patrolman had said. "The hi-jackers have a hide-out. When we're not on their trail, they slip off the road somewhere and wait until the coast is clear."

The bold tactics of the hi-jackers were of intense interest to the girls because of their own meeting with two of the men believed to be members of the gang.

Nor had Judy erased from her mind the fact that only a few hours earlier, she had seen the man she believed to be Joe Pompilli.

She was reflecting upon the matter as the station wagon driver let the girls off at Calico Cottage. Why, she wondered, had Lowell Diethelm been so certain that she was mistaken in the identification?

"He seemed honest enough in thinking that the man was a regular trucker on the road," she thought. "But if I were right, and Diethelm made a mistake—"

Her reflections were interrupted by Kathleen, who nudged her in the ribs.

"Why, so sober, Judy?"

"I was just speculating on those hi-jackers, Kathy," Judy replied as they started across the dew-laden lawn. "I'm more than half convinced that we made a bad mistake last night."

"You think we let Joe Pompilli get away?"

"We must have. Kathy, he and that other fellow we didn't know, may have been killing time at the restaurant, waiting for that truckload of auto parts to go through town! Then, they merely followed, and picked the truck off at a convenient spot on the road."

"That makes a nice sounding explanation," Kath-

AN URGENT CALL

leen chuckled. "But there's one bad flaw in your reasoning."

"Two of 'em," Judy admitted with a grin. "First, it doesn't seem logical that Joe Pompilli would dare show up in this area when he must know that state highway patrolmen are on the alert."

"He was badly hurt in that accident too," Kathleen added.

"Maybe not as seriously as we thought. The other defect in my theory is that Lowell Diethelm positively identified him as a regular trucker on the road."

"That's the part one can't get around," Kathleen nodded soberly. "Either, the patrolmen made a mistake in identifying an ordinary trucker as Joe Pompilli, or Lowell Diethelm has been misled."

"In either case, I guess it's too late for us to do anything about it now," Judy admitted. "We had our chance, and we muffed it."

Walking carefully so that they would not soak their shoes with the heavy dew, the girls tramped across the lawn to the back door of Calico Cottage.

Miss Meadows, who had seen them coming, flung open the door.

"I'm ashamed to have telephoned you," she apologized. "Have you had breakfast?"

"An early one," Judy replied as she and Kathleen entered the warm kitchen. "If those are muffins I smell, we can eat another one though!"

"Blueberry muffins," Miss Meadows smiled, peep-ing into the oven. "You arrived at just the right time, for they'll be done in three minutes."

"Aunt Mattie, why did you send such an urgent telephone message?" Judy asked abruptly. "You said it wasn't the ghost again."

"No, the basement was quiet enough last night."

"Then what did happen?"

"I know you think I'm nervous and silly—"

"No, such thing, Aunt Mattie."

"It was those lights that bothered me again. Now that it's morning, I feel much better about it. But last night, and until after I telephoned, I felt so jittery."

"Lights on the private road?" Judy questioned.

Miss Meadows did not answer until after she had removed the muffins from the oven. Then she said:

"I awoke about two o'clock, I'd judge. I can't explain it, but I had a strong feeling that something was wrong. I lay there in bed for awhile, listening. I could hear the muffled rumble of a big truck engine."

"Nothing so unusual about that, Aunt Mattie. A great many trucks pass on the main highway, even at night."

"This truck didn't pass," Miss Meadows said impressively. "I saw the lights flash past my bedroom window. Because I was nervous and couldn't sleep, I got up and looked out. I saw the truck stop, and the lights went off. Then the truck turned down that old road."

AN URGENT CALL

Judy and Kathleen had listened attentively to Miss Meadows' account. They exchanged a quick glance but remained silent.

"I suppose there's no occasion to be bothered about a truck turning down a private road," Judy's aunt chattered on. "It shouldn't worry me, I know. But I kept imagining all sorts of things, wondering if those men might be hi-jackers."

"Aunt Mattie, we don't consider you one bit silly to be nervous about it," Judy said quickly. "You didn't telephone the state highway patrol?"

"No, I thought of it, but after all, I didn't know but what the trucks had a right to be on that road. It could have been loggers?"

"How long did the truck remain on the private road?" Judy asked.

"So far as I know, it's still there. I sat up and watched until dawn. Since then, I've been rather busy."

"If the truck is still on that road, we should check—" Kathleen suggested quickly.

"I think we should," Miss Meadows agreed. "I'd have done it myself, only to tell you the truth, I was afraid to go alone."

"Who wouldn't be?" Judy backed her up. "When do we start? Right now?"

"No, finish your breakfast first," Miss Meadows urged. "Such nice muffins shouldn't be wasted."

Their thought on the investigation before them,

Judy and Kathleen ate quickly. Miss Meadows apologized for not having any milk to offer.

"I ran out yesterday," she remarked, "and the new milkman always comes very late."

"The new milkman?" Judy repeated, nearly dropping her knife. "What became of Bart?"

"I understand he's given up his job. The new man told me that Bart quit because of something special he wanted to do before the start of college."

"Something special," mused Judy. "You know what I think! Bart quit so he could thoroughly explore Calico Cave!"

"Oh, dear, I hope not," Miss Meadows murmured. "That sounds frightfully dangerous. You don't think he'd explore very far alone?"

"I certainly do," replied Judy. "From the little Bart said to me, I'm sure he hopes to solve the mystery of what became of his father. To do that, he'd have to brave the siphon."

"Gracious! I never heard of anything so reckless!" Miss Meadows gasped. "Why, the authorities shouldn't allow it!"

"I don't imagine Bart told anyone of his plan," Judy answered. "He's thoroughly familiar with the cave, and it would be safe enough for him to explore, providing he didn't try to go through the siphon."

"Just what is a siphon?" Miss Meadows inquired.

"Captain Hager said, a siphon is a tunnel through the cave, with a submerged ceiling. If one were a good swimmer, as Bart apparently is, one might dive and swim through it to open air on the other side."

"That's assuming that the tunnel wasn't very long," Miss Meadows commented.

"True," Judy nodded. "It would be a terrifying experience. Only a very courageous and foolhardy explorer would attempt it."

"Bart's just the type to risk it!" Kathleen asserted. "I wonder when he plans to tackle the siphon?"

"From what the new milkman told me, he may be in the cave even now!" Miss Meadows said with a shudder. "The mere thought of it frightens me."

"Bart knows how to take care of himself," Judy declared to relieve her aunt's mind somewhat. "I'm sure he does."

Breakfast over, Miss Meadows hastily cleared away the few dishes which had been used. She refused to let the girls wash them, insisting that she would stack them in the sink for a good soaking.

"Let's explore the road to the cave now," she urged. "I'll feel much better if I satisfy myself that everything is all right."

"We could call the Forest Service or one of the state highway patrolmen, if you'd rather," Kathleen proposed.

"If the truck shouldn't be there, or if it had a right to be, I'd never live down the mistake I'd made,"

Miss Meadows said. "No, I'd prefer to do a bit of checking for myself first."

She put on her heavy jacket as protection against the morning chill, and locked all the doors. The three then crossed the main highway and turned down the narrow rutty dirt road.

The sun was showing itself through the tall trees, as the explorers made their way down the steep slope. Almost at once, Miss Meadows triumphantly pointed to heavy tire tracks on the roadbed.

"See, I was right!" she exclaimed. "Those tire marks show that a big truck went down this road last night."

"Apparently only in one direction too," Judy agreed. "This road dead-ends, so either the truck had to turn around and come back, or it's still down there somewhere."

Quickening their pace, but becoming very quiet, the three moved on.

Presently they came to the end of the road.

"No truck here!" Kathleen exclaimed, halting.

"Here's where it made a turn," Judy said, pointing to deep tire marks in the road and grass.

Then she saw the truck itself. It had been driven entirely off the road and parked in a thick clump of bushes behind a shield of trees. Even so, the massive vehicle was only partially hidden from view.

While Kathleen and Miss Meadows waited tensely, Judy cautiously crept through the bushes to obtain a closer glimpse of the big truck.

AN URGENT CALL

The cab was deserted. Had the truck run out of gas perhaps, or was it being hidden there to escape detection?

Judy was quite certain she knew the answer, but to confirm her suspicions, she circled the transport. At the rear, she tried the big double doors which gave access to the cargo. They were locked.

Unable to learn more, she returned to report to her aunt and Kathleen.

"I'm convinced this is the truck that the highway patrolmen want to stop," she informed them. "After the road blocks have been removed, the hi-jackers may be able to slip out of here and get safely away!"

"Oh, no, they won't!" announced Miss Meadows with grim determination. "We'll tip off the state highway headquarters! I'll telephone."

"Someone should stay here to keep watch," Judy said. "The driver may return at any minute and try to pull out."

"That's so," Miss Meadows agreed. "I—I guess I'd better stay, while you girls telephone."

"No, you go to Calico Cottage," Judy urged. "Kathleen and I will wait here."

"You're not afraid?"

"No, you'll have help here in just a few minutes."

"I'll hurry as fast as I can," Miss Meadows promised, starting away. "Get into the bushes, and keep out of sight until I'm back here with the law!"

Chapter 19

THE HIDE-OUT

LEFT alone, Judy and Kathleen crept into the thicket at the left hand side of the road. The air was damp and chilly and leaves dripped moisture. In a very few minutes, the girls began to weary of crouching in such uncomfortable positions.

"That truck driver must have skipped out," Kathleen muttered. "It's sort of silly to hide here."

"I don't think so," Judy replied, keeping her voice low.

"I wish we knew where the driver went." Disregarding caution, Kathleen straightened up from her crouched position and carefully looked about.

She could see a portion of the trail which led toward Calico Cave. As she stood thus, a little dog came into view, trotting from the direction of the cavern.

"Why, it's Pete!" Kathleen exclaimed, speaking much louder than she had intended. "Do you suppose Bart is somewhere near, or in the cave?"

"He must be," Judy agreed. She added in warning: "But do quiet down. If we keep sounding off, we'll give our hiding place away to anyone who comes along."

THE HIDE-OUT

"Pete is onto it now!" Kathleen agreed in dismay.

The little dog had halted alertly on the trail. After sniffing the air, he left the path and came directly over to the bushes where the two girls had taken shelter.

To their consternation, he began to bark and to jerk his head, as if inviting them to follow him to the cave.

Judy seized the little dog, and tightly held his jaws so that he could not bark.

"This is a fine howdy-do!" she muttered. "Pete will give us away if anyone is within a mile of here!"

"Do you suppose Bart could be close?" Kathleen speculated. "Pete plainly is trying to get us to follow him to the cave."

"If we let him go, he'll set up a fearful clatter. I can't hold his jaws together forever either!"

"Bart would be a big help to us if we could find him."

"We could see if he's at the cave entrance," Judy said reluctantly. "I don't think we'll find him though, and we'd be leaving a good hiding place."

"We can be careful," Kathleen returned. "Help from the Forest Service or highway headquarters should be coming quite soon."

Allowing herself to be persuaded, Judy followed Kathleen from the leafy shelter. She kept tight hold of Pete however, not allowing him to bark or scramble out of her arms.

The rocky path wound through the trees and

around big boulders. Presently, the girls were within view of the dark entranceway to the cave.

Judy halted, thinking that she saw a tiny wisp of smoke emerging from the cavern. In that moment of inattention, Pete made a convulsive movement and before she could regain her grip, leaped to the ground.

Yipping excitedly, he ran toward the cave entrance.

With a gasp of dismay, Judy thrust Kathleen back into a thicket, and herself crouched behind a rock.

It was well that the girls took refuge, for Pete's loud barking had not gone unheard.

A dark figure appeared silhouetted in the opening of the cave. Judy could not see the face of the heavy-set man, but she knew instantly from his build that he was not Bart Ranieau.

"There's that confounded mutt again!" the girls heard the man exclaim. "He'll give us away!"

"Slug him with a rock!" came advice from inside the cave.

The man in the entranceway, heaved a stone which missed its mark by mere inches. Pete barked the louder.

"Put a bullet through him," was the next gruff advice.

"Don't dare," the girls heard the reply. "A shot would be heard too far."

"If we don't get out of this hole pretty soon, that

dog will have the whole town down on us," the other growled. "Quiet him somehow."

"Don't pay any attention to him and he'll shut up," the first man said. "If we can coax him in here, I'll wring his neck!"

Pete did stop barking after a few more excited yips, but canine caution kept him from going closer to the cave. In vain the two men tried to coax him into the cavern. Pete lay flat on his belly on the path and whined.

Finally, they abandoned the effort to get him inside, and themselves moved back out of view in the darkness.

For a long while, Judy and Kathleen remained motionless, afraid to stir lest they disclose their presence. Both were convinced that the two men in the cave were the hi-jackers, and that they merely were waiting there until they safely could move out their truck and stolen cargo.

"We can't stay here," Judy finally whispered to her chum. "Let's make a break for it. If we're seen, we'll have to run for our lives."

Moving stealthily, the girls slipped from their hiding place.

Pete saw them go and cocked his head attentively. But to their intense relief, he did not bark or try to follow them.

Safely, the girls retraced their way to the private road.

Once there, Judy anxiously looked up the slope

for a glimpse of her aunt or the assistance which she hoped would come.

"I guess we'll have to hide in the bushes again," Kathleen proposed. "Pete may ferret us out too."

As the girls debated what action to take, Judy saw that a green coupe had turned down the private road.

"A Forest Service car!" she exclaimed, over-joyed. "Good Aunt Mattie! She must have put through a fast telephone call to the ranger station. Our troubles are over!"

"I thought your aunt intended to call the highway patrol headquarters," Kathleen commented, watching the approaching car with troubled eyes.

"Maybe she called 'em both. At any rate, a forest ranger is just what the doctor ordered!"

Judy rushed out to meet the approaching automobile, waving her arms to attract attention.

The car drew up with a slight squeak of brakes. Judy saw then that the driver was Lowell Diethelm, and he seemed as surprised to see her and Kathleen as they were to encounter him on the lonely road.

"Did Aunt Mattie reach you?" Judy demanded.

The ranger's startled expression disclosed that he did not know what she was talking about.

"I guess Aunt Mattie hasn't had time to get word through," Judy went on. "Anyway, you're here in time to nab those hi-jackers!"

She and Kathleen then breathlessly told of their

suspicions, and pointed out the big truck which had been hidden in the thicket.

In their anxiety to tell the story clearly and fast, neither girl noticed that Diethelm was watching them in an odd sort of way, but not asking many questions.

When Judy finally ran out of breath, the ranger motioned for the two girls to get into the coupe.

"But aren't you going to do anything about it?" Judy demanded. "Don't you intend to find out if those men hiding in the cave are hi-jackers?"

"Sure, I intend to do something about it," Diethelm drawled, "but I'm not foolhardy. We're up against a tough gang. There may be shooting. I need reenforcements."

"I guess that's right," Judy agreed. Her gaze fell upon the radio equipment in the ranger's car. "Couldn't you call the ranger station?"

"Sure," Diethelm said again. "Sure. Come on, get in, and I'll take care of it."

Judy and Kathleen obeyed, sliding in beside the ranger. He turned the car around in the narrow roadway, heading it toward the main highway.

"I'll drive you up the hill," he said. "It's safer that way. Then if there should be shooting, you'll be all right."

"Can't we get word to the ranger station right away?" Judy urged again. "Those men may decide to try to pull out of here any minute."

"Take it easy," Diethelm advised. "Let me handle this, will you?"

"Sorry," Judy mumbled. "I didn't mean to suggest—only—"

"Only what?"

"Nothing," Judy replied shortly.

Diethelm reached across, snapping a lock on the door of the coupe. The gesture seemed careless enough. Yet, why should he have reason to lock the automobile? Judy, suddenly uneasy, glanced at Kathleen and saw that her chum looked frightened.

"So your aunt is telephoning the state highway patrol station?" the ranger remarked easily. "How long ago was that?"

"Five—maybe ten minutes ago," Judy answered. She was trying hard to smother the suspicion which had formed in her mind.

"Your aunt went to the cottage to phone?"

"Yes." Judy hesitated and then said earnestly: "Won't you please call ranger headquarters now on your radio telephone? It's important to get help fast. Aunt Mattie may have failed to get her call through."

Diethelm smiled and flipped a switch on the radio. He fumbled with it as he drove efficiently with one hand.

"Car 23 to Headquarters. Car 23 to Headquarters." he called.

"Go ahead, Diethelm," came the order from headquarters.

THE HIDE-OUT

"Nothing to report, sir. No fires sighted."

"Any sign of the hi-jackers? They're reported to have headed into your patrol area."

Diethelm spoke clearly and in a detached manner. "No sign of 'em anywhere," he replied. "Inform the highway patrol, they may as well lift the road block. That's right, sir. I've checked the area thoroughly. No sign of 'em."

Chapter 20

TREACHERY

JUDY and Kathleen scarcely could believe that they had heard the ranger's radio message correctly.

For a stunned moment, they sat in dead-silence, unable to comprehend what had transpired.

Diethelm wore the inconspicuous pine tree badge of the forest rangers, but he had never seemed friendly or helpful as had the other Forest Service men.

Judy had sensed the man's antagonism almost from the first moment of their meeting. Until this night, however, she had never actually distrusted him.

Now, as the meaning of his message to headquarters penetrated her brain, she realized that he deliberately had given false information to his superior officers. Information which would aid the hijackers, who awaited the lifting of the road block to rush their stolen cargo across the state line!

As the car climbed the steep incline, Kathleen suddenly reached for the door handle.

"I wouldn't do that!" Diethelm ordered sharply. "Stay in this car!"

"You're making us prisoners?" Kathleen gasped, shaken by the ranger's treachery.

"You asked for this," Diethelm retorted. "If you'd kept to your own affairs, no one would have bothered you. Now you've poked your pretty little noses in, you'll have to take the consequences!"

"Which are—?" interposed Judy. She was no longer frightened, but smoldered with a deep, burning anger.

"I'll drive you some distance from here and dump you in the woods," Diethelm informed her. "By the time you find your way out, we'll be over the state line. This is our last haul."

"So you're one of the hi-jackers!" Kathleen accused shrilly. "A disgrace to the ranger uniform!"

"I've not been in the service long," Diethelm said. "It means nothing to me. I adopted the uniform only to serve my own purpose. For six months it's been a cinch to run cargo through, but lately the state highway patrol has bottled up most of the roads. We'll move on to another state."

The car had reached the main highway. Judy could see Calico Cottage through the morning mist, but there was no sign of her aunt, or of any help.

Everything was painfully clear now! The Trucker she and Kathleen had seen the previous night at the restaurant, had indeed been Joe Pompilli. Either he, or his runners now were at the cave, awaiting a chance to slip their cargo over the state line. And with the road block soon to be lifted, that chance might come very soon!

The coupe turned onto the main highway, and started up the winding mountain road. Judy saw Diethelm glance anxiously at the gasoline gauge.

Her pulse leaped with hope, for she saw that the pointer already stood on the empty mark, and was giving only an occasional convulsive jerk.

"We're about out of gas," Diethelm muttered.

"No filling stations on this road for three miles," Judy said in satisfaction.

"We rangers have supply caches," Diethelm dashed her hopes again. "My own private one, is just ahead."

A few hundred yards farther up the road, he pulled off onto the right-of-way. Back among the trees, Judy and Kathleen saw the gasoline supply tank, marked with the Forest Service name.

Diethelm reached for a can on the floor behind the seat. As he got out of the car, he tapped the revolver in his holster.

"Now don't you move or try to get out of this car!" he ordered. "I'll have my eye on you. I'm warning that if you try to escape, I'll shoot.'

Diethelm then strode to the gasoline storage tank, hurriedly starting to fill his can.

"Lean forward—block off the window, so he can't see me," Judy instructed Kathleen tersely.

"He's watching us. If we try to get out, I'm afraid he'll carry out his threat to shoot."

TREACHERY

"We can't hope to get away," Judy admitted. "But theres one outside chance we can get through to ranger headquarters on the radio phone. I'm going to risk it."

Now that she knew her friend's scheme, Kathleen obediently shifted her position, so that her back temporarily shielded Judy from view.

In an instant, Judy had snapped the radio phone on.

"Car 23 to Headquarters!" she called excitedly into the transmitter. "Emergency call! Emergency call!"

"Headquarters to Car 23," came the reply. "Who the deuce is this? Diethelm—"

"I'm a Girl Scout—held a prisoner in Diethelm's car," Judy broke in. Aware that Diethelm himself had dropped the gasoline can and was striding toward the coupe, her words tumbled over each other in her haste to get them out. "The hi-jackers are at the cave! Their truck—"

The car door was jerked open at that point, and the radio phone ripped from Judy's hand, Diethelm clicked the switch off, pulling the girl bodily from the coupe.

"Now you've done it!" he snarled, shoving her so hard that she fell to the ground. "Little fool!"

Despite his previous threat, Diethelm did not touch his revolver. His face contorted by worry, he seemed uncertain what to do for a moment.

Tersely then, he ordered Kathleen out of the car also.

"Turn your backs and start walking into the woods," he ordered the two girls. "Keep walking. Don't look back or I'll shoot."

Kathleen pulled Judy to her feet, and they slowly moved off into the woods.

"Walk faster!" Diethelm shouted.

The girls obediently increased their speed, stumbling as they climbed over fallen logs and other forest debris.

Moments passed, and Judy dared to look over her shoulder. No longer could she see the car or the roadway.

But as she paused, she heard the roar of the coupe's engine.

"He's filled the gas tank and he's pulling out!" she declared. "Now to get help, if we can."

Hurrying back the way they had come, the girls reached the roadside in time to see the coupe disappearing around a curve in the direction from which it had come.

"He's going back to the cave to warn the hi-jackers!" Judy guessed shrewdly. "He must know I got through to the ranger headquarters!"

"Then that means that the hi-jackers probably will try to move their truck out now!" Kathleen exclaimed. "They may make it too, because it isn't far to the state line and the road block probably has been lifted."

"We must stop them somehow! Let's get back to Calico Cottage as fast as we can!"

They pounded down the road, hoping as they ran that a car would come along. None did. In Diethelm's coupe, the distance they had traveled from the junction with the private road had seemed very short. Now, the reverse was true.

Though the distance could not be more than a third of a mile, it seemed endless to the two Scouts. Alternately running and dog-trotting, they finally reached Calico Cottage, winded and perspiring.

As they crossed the yard, Miss Meadows came to meet them.

"I've had such a time," she began. "At first, I couldn't get my call through. Why, what's happened?"

Judy explained only briefly. She cut her story short by demanding: "Aunt Mattie, how soon do you think help will get here?"

"Ten minutes or longer. My call just went through. Before that the line was busy, and I couldn't get the operator to understand that this was an emergency!"

"Ten minutes!" Judy groaned. "That will give Diethelm all the time he needs to warn those men!"

"I saw a ranger car turn down the private road quite awhile ago," Miss Meadows contributed.

"That was Diethelm," Judy said desperately. "We've notified the ranger headquarters, but I doubt they can get men here quickly enough either!"

"If only we could block the private road somehow, so those hi-jackers can't get their truck out!" Kathleen exclaimed. "What could we use?"

Frantically, the three looked about the premises, but not an object was available which would offer an impediment to a powerful truck.

"The clothesline," Miss Meadows suggested doubtfully. "We could tie it to trees, across the road."

"It would snap in an instant," Judy said. "I doubt even a wire would delay them."

"Then there's nothing we can do," Miss Meadows said desperately. "Absolutely nothing."

"Nails?" proposed Kathleen. "We could throw them on the road and hope they'd spear the tires."

"There's a can of nails on the porch," Miss Meadows supplied eagerly. "The carpenter who must have built this cottage, apparently left them."

"It's an idea," Judy said slowly, "but it won't work. Those big truck tires would roll right over the nails without a puncture. Not even glass would cut them."

"I guess that's right," Miss Meadows admitted, crestfallen. "Oh, it's hopeless."

Judy, however, had a different idea. She was gazing speculatively at the "Welcome" mat on the doorstep.

"I think I know of a way to stop that truck if it tries to come through!" she cried. "My scheme is fantastic, but I'm sure it will work!"

Chapter 21

TRUCKER'S WELCOME

"HOW can we stop the truck if it tries to come through?" Kathleen demanded eagerly. "What is your idea, Judy?"

"You gave it to me yourself, when you mentioned dropping nails on the road," Judy answered. "That wouldn't do the trick, I'm sure, but I know what will! This rubber door mat!"

She stooped to pick up the dusty "Welcome" mat. As Kathleen and her aunt gazed at the object in bewilderment, she hastened to reveal what she had in mind.

"We can spear the nails through the mat so they'll stand upright! Then when the tires pass over them, they can't miss."

"That should do it!" Miss Meadows approved.

"Judy, you're a gem!" laughed Kathleen. "What a brain!"

"No brain, just a memory," Judy corrected. "I recall hearing a filling station serviceman relate how vandals once damaged big truck tires that way. I'm sure it will work if we can do it!"

"I'll get the nails," Miss Meadows said, starting away.

In a moment she returned with an assortment in a tin can. As fast as they could, the three puntured the rubber mat, forcing the nails through so that their sharp points were upright.

"Listen!" cried Judy suddenly.

She had heard the roar of a powerful motor starting far down the private road.

"It's the truck!" Kathleen exclaimed. "It's coming, and we don't have half enough nails in this mat!"

"There will be enough if the tires hit it," Judy declared. "The important thing is to get it placed, and fast! Come on!"

Without waiting for Kathleen or her aunt, she raced for the entrance to the private road.

She could not see the big truck which was hidden by the curves of the rutty thoroughfare, but she could tell from the roar of the engine, that it was coming as fast as it could climb the steep slope. Evidently, Diethelm had warned the hi-jackers, and knowing that delay would be fatal, they were making a run for it!

Judy had no time to deliberate where she would lay the mat. She dropped it on the right hand side of the road, directly across an old truck track.

If the driver saw the mat, he could swerve to miss it. She was depending though upon the sharp curve, figuring that the truck would come around it fast, and that the big transport would roll over the nails before they could be seen.

TRUCKER'S WELCOME

Kathleen and Miss Meadows already had screened themselves behind the bushes lining the private road. Judy scarcely had time to slide in beside them, when the massive transport careened around the curve.

The front wheel struck a deep rut and the truck veered from the middle of the road.

"They're going to miss it!" Kathleen moaned, gripping Judy's arm so hard that is hurt.

But the next moment, the driver brought the truck back onto its course. Apparently, he had failed to see the studded mat lying directly in the path. Both front and rear tires rolled over the long, sharp nails.

Breathlessly, the three watchers waited. Nothing seemed to happen.

Then the huge truck reached the entrance to the private road, there was a loud hissing of air. The transport began to wobble crazily. First the front tire went down and then the one at the right rear.

"We've done it!" Judy laughed jubilantly. "We've stopped them!"

"But for how long?" Miss Meadows speculated. "Don't move, girls! Keep hidden! Those men are in an ugly mood."

The two hi-jackers had leaped from the cab of the crippled truck. As they beheld the disaster which had befallen them, a car came up the hill, pulling alongside. It was the Forest Service automobile, driven by Lowell Diethelm. By mere inches, the tires missed the nail-studded rubber mat.

"Now what?" the ranger demanded furiously. "Can't you keep going and get out of here?"

"Keep going?" one of the truckers snarled. "On rims? We'll have to abandon the cargo." Diethelm swung open the door of the coupe. "Get in!" he directed. "We'll try to get over the state line.

The possibility of the two hi-jackers transferring to the ranger's car had not occurred to Judy. Now, convinced that her scheme had failed, she involuntarily started to leave her hiding place.

Miss Meadows held her back. "No, Judy!" she warned. "We've done all we can! Those men are dangerous. Let them go."

"Let them go," Judy half moaned. "Oh, this is awful! After stopping that big truck, to fail so miserably!"

"We saved the cargo at any rate," Kathleen reminded her. "Furthermore, Diethelm hasn't driven off yet! I don't think he will either!"

The latter excited comment was made as she saw two Forest Service cars sweep down the main highway.

Before Loell Diethelm could pull away, the other two automobiles had blocked the main highway.

"Our fish are netted now!" Kathleen shouted gleefully. "Who says your idea failed, Judy? It was a grand one!"

No longer fearful, the three came out of hiding.

Six rangers, two of whom the Scouts knew by sight, had surrounded Lowell Diethelm's car. They had their revolvers trained on the two hi-jackers, but Diethelm was trying to put up a convincing story.

"I captured these birds red-handed," he said glibly. "I was trying to get 'em to headquarters, when they over-powered me. I'm sure glad you fellows came along."

"Yeah?" dryly inquired Ranger Wentz. "Sounds pretty phoney, Diethelm. You'll have to think up a better one than that to tell the chief."

By this time, Judy, Kathleen and Miss Meadows had reached the ranger cars. As rapidly as they could talk, they told the Forest Service men exactly what had occurred.

"You're the girl who called over the radio phone, aren't you?" one of the rangers asked Judy.

"That's right.'

"She stopped the truck too, by putting nails on the road," Kathleen added, very proud of her friend. "What a 'welcome' that mat proved to be for the hi-jackers!"

Within five minutes, the rangers were reenforced by state highway patrolmen, who had responded to an alert. If there had been any previous doubt as to the identity of the two hi-jackers, it then was dispelled. State highwaymen definitely identfied Joe Pompilli, and recognized his companion as

Porky Burns, a hi-jacker, who had operated in three states.

"Five or six drivers work this area," a ranger told Judy. "Joe's the head of the outfit though. We may never catch the others, but now that we have him, the gang will fall apart."

"Joe was pretty reckless to keep working this territory after he knew he was wanted," Judy remarked. "Especially after that truck accident, when Kathy and I patched him up."

"Joe operates that way," the ranger answered. "He was dead sure of himself. First, he could depend upon our double-crossing friend, Diethelm, to tip him off as to road blocks."

"This private road to the cave must have been used in emergencies too," Judy added. My aunt saw the truck headlights on one of the nights that the state highway patrol had put up its road block."

"Sure," the ranger agreed, "it's plain enough that Diethelm tipped 'em off regularly. That's probably why they chanced making one last haul before they moved to another locality. Pompilli had taken pains to make himself known as a regular trucker on the road, especially at Silverton and Grove City where he was a good spender. He figured only the state highway patrol could cause him any trouble, and he took that chance."

The state patrolmen requested Kathleen and Judy to accompany them to headquarters to make sworn statements as to their knowledge of what had happened. Eager to pin evidence on the two men, they went willingly. They were questioned at length, and in turn learned considerably more about how Joe Pompilli and his gang had operated.

"Without Diethelm's help, we'd have cleaned them out weeks ago," a patrolman told the Scouts. "He's made a clean breast of his part in the mess to the chief forester."

"Diethelm has confessed?" Kathleen asked in disbelief.

"Yes, he knew we had him dead to rights anyway. Matter of fact, he's rather remorseful, the boys tell me. Diethelm's a queer duck. It seems he made a brilliant record in college and had a fine career ahead of him as a forest ranger. But on his first assignment, something went wrong. He ran into personal trouble with his superior, and was reprimanded. He couldn't take it. So he brooded and figured on a way to get even."

"Then the help he gave the hi-jackers was to even an old score with another ranger?" Judy inquired.

"Not entirely. It made him susceptible to suggestion, shall we say. Diethelm was a weak character. He wanted easy money. Joe Pompilli offered it to him, and so he sold himself cheap."

"Diethelm even accused the girls in our Scout Camp of being careless with fire," Kathleen remarked indignantly.

"Oh, that matter came up," the highway patrolman said, reminded of it by her remark. "Diethelm admitted to the chief ranger that on two occasions he started small fires as a diversion. He wanted to keep rangers and patrolmen occupied to give the hi-jackers a better chance to slide their stolen cargo through."

"Then the Scouts can't be blamed for that fire?"

"No, they've been cleared."

"Well, that's a relief!" Kathleen laughed.

"There's one thing that puzzles me," Judy said thoughtfully. "When my aunt first moved into Calico Cottage, someone telephoned—"

"I can tell you about that too," the patrolman broke in. "Krumm's cottage stood idle for quite a spell. Now and then, Diethelm or members of Joe's gang would use the telephone. The cottage gave a clear view of the entrance to the private road. A couple of times, we think Joe and his truckers spent a night at the cottage. Naturally, after your aunt moved in, they had to abandon using it."

"Maybe that explains the ghost!" Kathleen exclaimed.

Judy, however, shook her head. "I'm afraid not," she said. "At least I haven't heard that Joe Pompilli played a flute. Our ghost is an entirely different matter."

By the time the two girls returned to Calico Cottage, it was well after eleven o'clock. Miss Meadows anxiously awaited their return. She listened attentively to their long account of what had happened in town.

"I'm glad that's over and we won't be bothered by weird lights on the road any more," she declared fervently. "If I weren't so worried about Bart, I could begin to enjoy my vacation here."

"Bart?" Judy repeated, startled. The excitement of the morning had washed all thought of the young milkman from her mind.

"I took it upon myself to telephone his landlady," Miss Meadows went on. "Bart left his room early yesterday morning, and he's not been seen since!"

"That might not mean anything serious, Aunt Mattie."

"I talked with the other milkman this morning while you were in town," Miss Meadows continued. "He thinks as I do, that Bart went into the cave."

"Maybe he went down into the cavern before those hi-jackers parked themselves in the entranceway," Kathleen speculated. "Perhaps he didn't dare come out until they left. He may be waiting somewhere in the dark passageway even now."

"That is a possibility," agreed Miss Meadows, instantly becoming more cheerful. She reached for her hat and jacket. "I'll go down there now, and let him know that it's safe to come out."

Chapter 22

DESCENT INTO THE CAVE

JUDY and Kathleen would not allow Miss Meadows to go alone to Calico Cave.

Insisting upon accompanying her, they made cheerful talk as they tramped down the now familiar forest road.

Moving along the narrow path far above the silvery white river, Judy was the first to see Pete lying at the mouth of the dark cave.

"Why, he's still there!" she exclaimed. "Poor doggie, do you suppose he's had anything to eat or drink?"

Pete lay upon his stomach, head between his paws. A picture of utter dejection, he whined and whimpered as the girls stooped to pet him.

"Bart must be down in the cave," Judy declared. "Otherwise, why would Pete lie here and act as if he'd lost his last friend?"

The three stepped into the dim interior of the cave. Judy cupped her hands and shouted Bart's name repeatedly.

Her voice echoed weirdly through the cave, but there was no answering call. If Bart had descended into the cavern, it was evident that he was at a level so far below that he could not hear the cry.

"No, Judy," Miss Meadows said firmly, as her niece would have started down into the cave. "We don't dare explore alone. It's unsafe."

"What should we do?" Kathleen asked, pulling her jacket more tightly about her, for the air was cool.

"Bart may be safe enough," Judy added anxiously. "Then again, if he braved the siphon, there's no telling what may have happened."

"I'll get in touch with Bart's landlady again," Miss Meadows finally decided. "There's a chance he may have gone out of town, and returned to his room by this time."

"If he shouldn't be back—" Judy began. "Then what?"

"I don't know what we can do except to notify the authorities," Miss Meadows said, deeply troubled. "Meanwhile, you girls are to return to camp. I'll feed Pete and see if I can coax him to the cottage."

"I don't feel like going back to camp just now," Judy said soberly. "Until I know that Bart is safe, I couldn't enjoy any of the Scout activities."

"Neither could I," chimed in Kathleen. "It's been such an exciting day already. I feel sort of jitterey inside."

The three crawled out of the cave into the sunlight. Pete scrambled up alertly as they emerged, but could not be coaxed away from the entranceway.

"If only we dared go down into the cave, we could learn what became of Bart," Kathleen remarked to her companions who stood silent and uncertain. "Then we could end this dreadful suspense."

"We can't go down into the cave without a guide," Miss Meadows repeated firmly. "I know of no one—"

"Captain Hager!" Judy cried. "He could help us, if he will!"

"Of course! Why didn't I think of him? At the very least, he should be able to advise us. Where does he live, Judy?"

"I'm not sure. I think, in a cabin somewhere along the river."

"Do you suppose you girls could find him?" Miss Meadows urged. "I'll wait here."

"We can try,' Judy promised.

She and Kathleen set off at once, making their way to the river level. Captain Hager was not at the dock where they first had met him, nor was his boat anywhere visible on the river.

Judy surveyed the water front, noticing a two-room shack several hundred yards down the beach.

"That might be his place," she said. "We can try there anyway."

A brisk walk brought them to the modest little cabin. Though small, the building was trim and

DESCENT INTO THE CAVE 195

neat, and had recently been whitewashed. There was a little garden at the rear, carefully watered and fertilized. An anchor, encrusted with rust, hung above the door.

"This must be Captain Hager's place," Judy decided.

She knocked. After a time, the door opened. Captain Hager stood there in his shirt sleeves, looking older and less spry than the girls had remembered him.

But upon recognizing the Scouts, his face creased into a welcoming smile.

"Come in, come in!" he boomed.

The room into which he led the girls was extremely severe and quite bare of furniture. There was a bunk bed, a stove, an ice box and two wooden chairs. Above the bed hung the picture of a middle-aged woman in a heavy gilt frame.

"My wife," said Captain Hager, noticing Judy's eyes upon the picture. "That was all I kept from the old place. Sold all my furniture at auction. An old salt like me can't be bothered with fancy trappings."

He limped as he walked across the cabin floor to pull out chairs for the girls.

"Your leg is bothering you?" Judy asked, taking the seat he offered.

"Oh, it's the old rheumatiz come back to fret me," Captain Hager sighed. "For the last couple o' days I've been hobbling around like a cripple."

Judy gazed at Kathleen despairingly, feeling that it would be useless even to broach the subject of the call. In seeking Captain Hager as a guide, she had forgotten that his lively talk and manner belied his age and infirmities.

"Now what brings you here?" the captain inquired. "If it's fishing, I'll have to say no, because I'm in dry dock for a couple of days until I get to feeling better again."

"We didn't know about your rheumatism," Judy said. "I guess it's quite out of the question."

"What is?" the old man demanded. "It wasn't fishing that brought you here"

Judy shook her head. "Its Bart," she told him. "We think he's gone into the cave again. He's been missing more than a day, and we're afraid he's trapped down there. Either that, or he's attempted the siphon."

Captain Hager did not speak for a long while. Then he muttererd: "The siphon! I told that boy to wash it out of his mind, but I always knew he'd try it someday. The thought of it always was a challenge and a plague to him."

"What do you think we should do?" Judy asked desperately. "Notify the authorities?"

"If he's gone through the siphon, he's beyond help," the old man answered. "There's no man living in this community, who would risk his life to try to force that tunnel of water. Either he'll get back on his own, or like his father before him, he'll be heard of no more."

DESCENT INTO THE CAVE

"But supposing he didn't attempt the siphon," Kathleen interposed. "Maybe he's trapped somewhere below the surface by a fall of rock. Would the rangers check, do you think?"

"They might make up a search party," the old man conceded. "But who would lead it? That cave is as simple as A-B-C for a skipper that knows the layout. The rangers have their maps, but what do they know of Hager's Hole? Now if I were ten years younger—"

"It wouldn't be fair to ask you," Judy said, "You're not feeling well and your rheumatism—"

"Who says I'm not feeling well?" Captain Hager growled. "Next to good salt air, there's nothing better for the ache o' old bones than cool cave air."

"You'll take us down there?" Judy asked eagerly. "You're sure it wouldn't be too hard on you?"

"I'll go as far as the siphon, or until we find Bart," the old captain promised.

"How soon can we get started?" Judy urged.

"As soon as I gather some rope, a good light and a few things we may need. But time's no matter in a cave. Night or day, it's all the same, once you're underground."

"Will we need heavy clothes?" Kathleen asked.

"Those you're wearing will be all right," the captain assured her. "The temperature is the same everywhere in the cave. Heavy clothing is cumbersome and burdens one in climbing. You'll need flashlights and plenty of extra batteries."

Chapter 23

THE SIPHON

THE descent to the chamber of the White Witch was quickly made. There, the party of three paused briefly to catch breath and to view again the weird figure which captured the imagination.

A tunnel, at times narrow and low, wound deeper and deeper into the earth. Judy and Kathleen kept close to their guide. In the stillness of the cavern they could hear his somewhat labored breathing, for even the slightest sound was magnified.

They came presently to another small chamber where they paused, speechless. Stalactites sparkled like jewels, standing out in the most fantastic shapes.

Judy could imagine animal figures, all in a variety of color, milky white, red, green and black. The colors, Captain Hager explained, came from mineral infiltration.

"No wonder Bart couldn't resist this cave," Judy remarked in awe, entranced. "It's like a fairyland! How I wish all the Scouts could see it!"

In close formation, the three went on into the cavern depths. A cooler wind met them, but from where it arose they gained no clue.

The going had become harder now, and after

edging through a narrow space, the three stopped for a moment beside a translucent column which rose from the floor to the roof.

As they stood thus, there came a deafening crash behind them.

Judy and Kathleen froze in their tracks, too terrified to utter a sound.

"A cave-in behind us?" Kathleen finally asked in a choked whisper.

"It's nothing," the captain reassured her. "Sounded like a blast of dynamite far away. Like enough the rangers are blasting a tree stump somewhere in the park area."

"But it sounded as if the cave roof had fallen!" Judy said, still shaken.

"All sounds underground are magnified," Captain Hager explained. "Even the dripping of water can be very loud. Off to the right there is a Talking Grotto. But we will not explore that passage, for Bart would not waste time there."

To proceed, it was necessary to creep across a slippery formation which resembled a frozen waterfall. They passed through a room which was cluttered with grotesque toadstool types of stalagmites, and then came to formations so delicate that they appeared as a lacy cobweb.

As they sat down to rest their legs for a moment, Captain Hager told the girls that the beautiful pillars they had seen farther back were made by the joining of stalactites and stalagmites.

The growth of formations, he added, was much faster than generally believed. Varying rainfall, the thickness of the rock penetrated by water, and the rate of drip, all affected the deposits, he explained.

"All water that goes into a cave, must come out somewhere," the captain continued. "During a hard rain storm, this cave could be dangerous at the lower levels."

"You mean we'd get the rain down here?" Kathleen questioned in amazement.

"Belatedly, yes. Shortly now, you'll see the underground river. During the dry months it shrivels, but in the rainy season, it thunders through the chasms like a mad demon."

"I hope it doesn't storm today," Kathleen said nervously.

"The day was clear," Captain Hager reassured her. "And there has been no recent rain to flood the underground stream."

Farther on, the girls came to a series of small pools in which there were blind fish. They did not tarry long, but continued through another long, narrow passage.

"Do you suppose Bart came this way?" Judy finally asked. "Couldn't he have taken any number of branch-offs?"

"The branch-offs are dead-end streets, so to speak," replied the captain. "If I know that lad, we'll find him at the siphon, or we'll not find him this voyage. Tired?"

THE SIPHON

"My legs feel sort of cramped," Judy confessed, ashamed of her weariness. "But I'm all right."

"We're nearing the end," the captain encouraged the girls. "The last few yards are the hardest. Then we'll bring up at the siphon."

"And if Bart isn't there?" asked Judy.

The old captain did not answer. He gazed thoughtfully at his sturdy boots, tested his light briefly on the limestone wall, and then signaled that he was ready to resume the descent.

Not far beyond the point where they had rested, the three explorers came to a chamber so large that it seemed to have no surrounding walls.

At its entrance, Captain Hager hesitated, seemingly reluctant to go on.

"If we continue to the siphon, we must cross this chamber, with no wall to guide us," he explained. "Beyond, in the darkness, there is a single narrow passageway leading on. If we hit the target, we'll soon be at the end of the cave. If we miss, we may spend hours, trying to grope our way. We'll be like a ship wallowing without chart or compass. Unless you have plenty of nerve—"

"We have," Judy said resolutely. "We've come so far now, we can't turn back without learning whether or not Bart is in the cave."

"Aye, I figured you'd say that," Captain Hager replied.

He then uncoiled a length of nylon rope, tying it first about his own waist, then around Kathleen, and finally about Judy, who would bring up the rear.

"We must keep close together," he warned. "If we do, there is no danger. Even if we miss the passageway on the first try, we will find it. Full steam ahead, my hearties!"

For a few feet the girls followed along a rough, jagged wall before moving slowly out into the vast room. The silence and immensity of the cavern were momentarily terrifying, for Captain Hager's light revealed only a dark void ahead.

By supreme effort Judy and Kathleen held their nerves in rigid check. Each step seemed to be taking them deeper and deeper into oblivion. A dozen doubts assailed them. Would Captain Hager ever find the narrow passage leading out of the chamber? And if they should be successful in reaching the siphon, would not the return be even more difficult?

The darkness seemed endless, but finally Captain Hager's light revealed a rough wall ahead. A wave of relief washed over Judy and Kathleen. But it was short lived.

Their guide had paused to move the flash beam slowly along the solid wall, first to the right, then to the left. He muttered something, but his words were indistinguishable.

"Are—are we lost?" Kathleen asked.

The captain deliberately did not answer. After a moment, he started on again, groping along the wall. Kathleen did not repeat her question.

For awhile Captain Hager kept on, the girls directly behind, following blindly. Then suddenly the old man seemed to relax, and they heard him give a throaty chuckle.

"Hear that?" he demanded.

Judy and Kathleen already had distinguished the distant sound of running water. The underground stream!

At the same instant that they heard the splash of water, Captain Hager's flash beam focused upon the narrow opening in the cavern wall—the passageway for which he had searched.

"We near the end," he said simply.

They moved quickly through the narrow corridor. The thunder of a distant waterfall they never were to see, was louder now in their ears.

The floor of the passageway sloped sharply downward. Kathleen slipped but did not fall, for Judy caught her arm to give her support.

Abruptly, the corridor turned, and the girls saw water ahead. The underground stream, quiet and dark, emerged from a wall of rock to flow tranquilly beneath the slightly arched cave-roof above.

Captain Hager halted. "We've come to the end," he announced.

Judy and Kathleen were stunned. "The end," Judy repeated, scarcely comprehending. "But I thought—"

"We can proceed no further without wading

along the river bed," the captain explained. "The water gradually deepens until it rises to the ceiling. At that point, one must dive through and swim underwater, or turn back."

He focused his light to the right, and the girls saw the meeting place of wall and water.

"The siphon?" Judy asked.

"Aye, how far it goes, no man knows. It may extend for only a few feet or yards. Then again, it may run on indefinitely, with nary a pocket of air."

"Bart—?" Judy hesitated to ask the question that was foremost in her mind.

"Surely he wouldn't be crazy enough to try to swim through the siphon!" Kathleen exclaimed.

"The lad is a true spelunker, like his father. He has the courage of a lion, and the muscles of a young bear. Since he was a mere boy, he's studied and dreamed about this cave."

"But we've seen no evidence that he's anywhere in the cavern," Judy said hopefully.

"No evidence?" Captain Hager's voice was muted, as his light came to focus upon a rock shelf a few feet above the river bed.

For a moment, neither Judy nor Kathleen understood.

Then, they fully comprehended. There on the rock ledge, set heel to hell, was an empty pair of shoes. Beside them, in a neat roll, was Bart's shirt and jacket.

Chapter 24

HELP FROM CAPTAIN HAGER

THREE hours now had elapsed since Captain Hager, Judy and Kathleen had ascertained that Bart Ranieau was somewhere deep in the cave, beyond the siphon.

Unable to penetrate farther, the three had made the arduous climb back to the cavern entrance where Miss Meadows anxiously awaited them.

Their report had been a discouraging one. Without question, Bart was somewhere in Calico Cave, but whether or not alive, no one could say.

"The lad may have reached an air pocket, or a chamber," Captain Hager said. "That's what he gambled on."

"He's been missing a day and a half now," Miss Meadows reminded the seaman. "While you were down in the cave, I checked on that point. Surely, if he's ever coming back, he'd have made it by now."

"Aye," the captain soberly agreed.

"Can't something be done?" Miss Meadows urged.

"Not a man in these parts would risk that siphon, ma'am."

"I realize that," Miss Meadows answered. "But is there no other way to reach him, if he's still alive? Couldn't the rangers blast the rock perhaps?"

"It would be impractical and dangerous, Ma'am."

"But the cave must have an exit somewhere close —if only it could be traced down! If one could approach the siphon from the other direction—"

"Aye, Ma'am," Captain Hager replied, "I've been pondering on it—pondering hard."

"Then you do have an idea!" Judy cried. "Does it have anything to do with Calico Cottage?"

"I've been meditatin' along that line," the old man admitted.

"Is there any chance the cave connects in some way with the foundation of the cottage?" Judy demanded excitedly. "Remember, all those strange sounds which seemed to come from the basement! They might have been cave noises! And we noticed a gust of cool air coming through a crack in the mortar."

"Aye," the captain nodded. "Bart and I discussed it many a time. Those strange sounds that have scared the living daylights out of cottage tenants come from the cave right enough."

"Then there must be a passageway close to the foundation wall!" Judy cried.

"I tried to convince Krumm he should build on a new foundation, but he wouldn't take advice."

"If that old foundation could be torn down, maybe an opening down into the cave could be found!"

Judy went on. "What do you think, Captain Hager?"

"It's our only chance to ever learn what became of Bart."

"Then why are we waiting?" Miss Meadows demanded. "We must put men to work at once!"

"Krumm will have to give his permission," Captain Hager said, deeply troubled. "It will mean wrecking the foundation of the cottage."

"But a young man's life is at stake!"

"Aye," the captain agreed. "Krumm should consent, if there's a mite o' humanity in him. We'll go now and put it up to him."

Word had spread through the village of Bart Ranieau's plight and everyone, it seemed, was discussing the young man's fate. Even before the little party arrived at Mr. Krumm's real estate office, groups of curious began to congregate at the cave entranceway.

Forest rangers and state highwaymen roped off the private road leading to the cavern, and set up guards to prevent persons from trying to explore. Miss Ward, bringing her girls to Calico Cottage, learned belatedly of the disaster and what was being done to try to find Bart.

Meanwhile, Captain Hager was using all his powers of persuasion upon Mr. Krumm. The real estate man, reluctant to have his property damaged, argued that it would be a useless expenditure to tear down the old foundation wall.

"Like as not we wouldn't find the cave exit," he protested. "Even if we did, there's not much chance of finding that foolhardy young man alive and you know it! He went the way his father did before him, drowned in the siphon!"

"We don't know it," Captain Hager retorted. "There's air somewhere close by to that siphon."

"How do you know?"

"Because time and again Bart found tadpoles."

"What have they got to do with it?" Mr. Krumm demanded.

"Tadpoles are a sure sign of open air being near. They're creatures that never venture far into underground waters."

"So?"

"I figure there must be a brook somewhere close where the underground river empties."

"There's no brook around the cottage, and no water under it either."

"I'm not concerned where the river empties," Captain Hager said. "I do think the cottage wall connects in some way with a passage down into the cave. Where it would lead, if we get into it, no man knows."

"You want me to tear down the foundation on a wild chance like that?"

"You've got to do it," Captain Hager said grimly. He moved in close. "Either you do it like a gentleman and get credit for being a hero, or I'll have the

HELP FROM CAPTAIN HAGER

law on you! You can't abandon that boy to save a dollar!"

Mr. Krumm's eyes snapped angrily. Judy and Kathleen were certain he would order them all out of the real estate office.

But suddenly, his opposition dissolved.

"Okay, tear down the foundation!" he consented. "Get on with it!"

Once Mr. Krumm had waived his objection, men from the village, directed by forest rangers, immediately went to work.

Judy, Kathleen and the other Scouts milled about the cottage, watching as a small section of the foundation was torn apart. As the throng increased, only Miss Meadows, Miss Ward and the Scouts were permitted in the building.

Dust from the bricks and mortar kept the girls out of the cellar much of the time. But as the day wore on, a shout from below, brought them scrambling down the stairway.

By this time, one section of wall had been torn away, though the main supports of the cottage remained. The musty odor which had annoyed occupants of Calico Cottage now was very strong and definitely came from the jagged opening. A group of workmen clustered about the hole, blocking Judy's view.

"Have you found the cave opening?" she cried. "Have you?"

"Aye," Captain Hager informed her jovially. "But where the passage leads, we don't know."

"What causes the odor?" Kathleen asked, sniffing.

"Imprisoned air. It's gradually clearing out. Like as not it comes from decaying vegetation—"

"Listen!" cried Judy tensely.

"The boy with the flute!" exclaimed Kathleen in awe.

Those in the room had frozen to attention. From the great gaping hole there issued forth a musical note, for all the world like the music of a flute.

Then there came a series of taps as if someone might be thumping a stick on hard rock.

"That's a man-made sound!" cried Captain Hager. "Bart's down there! He's trying to signal us!"

"We'll get him out!" shouted a forest ranger. "Any volunteers to go down into the hole?"

Arthur Wentz stepped forward. Rope was tied about his waist, and carefully he was lowered until his feet touched solid floring.

For awhile those above could see the descending light, then it vanished. They paid out more and more rope until the coil was nearly exhausted.

Finally, a signal came—two short tugs. Gently, the men began to pull on the rope.

"Wentz is coming up!" one of the workmen shouted. "It's hard pulling!"

"Then he must have found Bart!" Judy cried, hugging Kathleen in her excitement.

HELP FROM CAPTAIN HAGER

Minutes passed as the men kept at the rope. Then from the hole staggered Wentz and the young man he supported.

Bart was barefoot and his bare back had been covered by the ranger's shirt. His lips were blue with cold, but he grinned with the spirit of a conqueror.

"Captain Hager!" he mumbled, embracing the old man. "I did it!"

"You sure did, son," the captain answered, tears streaming down his grimy cheeks. "You almost did for yourself too."

"I thought you'd get me out," Bart said. "I never gave up, never for a minute."

"You can thank these Scouts," Captain Hager said, smiling at Judy and Kathleen. "They pested me to go down into the cave with 'em. If they hadn't, we'd never have learned that you went through the siphon."

"It was a wonderful but terrifying experience," Bart mumbled. "My father—"

"That can wait," Captain Hager said gruffly. "You can tell us all about it later. Get yourself to a warm bed now, before you die of pneumonia. Get along with ye!"

Nearly exhausted, and shaking with cold, Bart was lifted bodily and carried to a waiting ambulance.

Chapter 25

COURT OF HONOR

TWO days had elapsed since Bart Ranieau had been brought out of Calico Cave suffering from shock, but otherwise unharmed by his thrilling explorations.

Long hours of sleep and plenty of food had restored him to his former peak of health. But as his strength returned, he became restless and pestered hospital officials until at last they dismissed him.

Almost immediately, Bart sought Judy and Kathleen at Pine Cone Camp to thank them for saving his life.

Word spread like wildfire that the young explorer had arrived and soon the daring young man was surrounded by Girl Scouts who teased him to tell the story of his adventure.

"Start at the very beginning," Judy urged. "Don't leave out anything.'

"That's a large order, but I'll try," grinned Bart. "Well, I'd made up my mind to try the siphon. I didn't tell anyone, because I knew if I did, the authorities would try to stop me."

"I left my shoes and shirt on the ledge because I couldn't be burdened with them in swimming. I reasoned too, that if I got through, wet clothes wouldn't help keep me warm. So I stripped to my trunks."

"How long was the siphon?" inquired Betty Bache, who had joined the group of intent listeners.

"Long enough," Bart said grimly. "The first one wasn't so bad."

"Then there was more than one?" inquired Ardeth Packett.

"Two of them. I waded at first. The water finally came up to my neck and then over my nose. When I couldn't walk, I dived."

"Weren't you scared to death?" Virginia Cunningham asked with a shiver.

"I sure was," Bart admitted. "I knew I might find water to the ceiling for an indefinite distance ahead. Anyway, I decided to chance it. I took a great deep breath and plunged through."

"What happened?" questioned Beverly Chester breathlessly.

"The first barrier was astonishingly easy. I was through it in less than a minute and was able to wade again. My only light was a container of matches carried in the top of my bathing cap. Ahead I could see another siphon."

"You were reckless to go on," Kathleen chided.

"Maybe," Bart acknowledged, "but it would have been very nearly as hard to have gone back. I hoped I'd find where the cave came out."

"Tell us about the second siphon," Judy urged.

"It was a tricky one, I'm here to report. I don't know how long I was underwater, but it seemed a minute and a half. My lungs were bursting when finally I emerged. But it was worth it!"

"What did you find?" demanded Beverly.

"A hall filled with the most beautiful formations I've ever seen."

"Better than the White Witch and those chambers before one gets to the siphon?" Judy asked.

"Oh, a thousand times better! I stood there speechless and in awe, dazzled by the glitter of so much crystal. For a little while, I lost all count of time. It seemed unreal."

"Go on," Kathleen urged, as Bart became lost in his own memories.

"Those stalactites and mites were fantastic beyond description," Bart told the Scouts. "There were animal shapes, and statue-like figures—one a woman with a bridal veil. Why, if steps can be built down from Calico Cottage, everyone can see the chamber! Krumm will make more money opening up the cave than he ever could do renting the cottage."

"While you were down there, you didn't solve the mystery of Calico Cave's ghost, did you?" Judy asked. "You didn't meet our little boy with the flute?"

"I certainly did," Bart replied. "The explanation for those flute noises is simplicity itself. One of the roof formations takes the shape of a long hollow tube. Each time water drops through the tube onto the floor, it produces the musical note."

"Did you realize how close you were to the basement of Calico Cottage?" Judy next asked the young explorer.

"I thought I might be somewhere near, but I couldn't be sure. One loses all sense of direction under ground. I tried to climb, but the rocks were straight up, and I couldn't get a grip."

"When you first came out of the cave, you spoke of your father," Kathleen said, rather reluctant to remind Bart of a painful subject.

"Yes, I know now what became of him," he answered. "My father didn't drown as we thought. He made both of the siphons just as I did."

"Then he was trapped in the chamber and unable to signal anyone."

"I'm not sure if he tried or had the strength to signal," Bart responded. "I found the skeleton and a note, only part of which I've been able to read. My dad had a heart attack. He wasn't too expert as a swimmer, and the exertion together with the excitement of his discovery, may have brought on a sudden attack. It must have taken him fast."

"But there was no escape from the chamber?" Virginia probed. "No way back?"

"Of that I'm not sure either," Bart returned. "It would take a hardy swimmer to swim against the current. I think I might have made it. I was turning the thought over, trying to decide what to do. I'd about made up my mind that if no help came, I'd attempt it before my strength left me."

"Does the cave have no exit except through the cottage foundation?" Ardeth next interposed a question. "What becomes of the underground river?"

"It empties into the brook which flows into the river," Bart explained. "But no one can follow the course of the underground stream farther than I went. The way beyond is barred by solid rock."

The young explorer spent more than an hour at camp, telling the Scouts many interesting facts about caves in general.

All the girls were envious of Judy and Kathleen because they had viewed so many of the beautiful formations.

"The most breath-taking sights are in the chamber directly under Calico Cave," Bart said. "There's no reason why a ladder or steps can't be built down there, so everyone can view them. I am to talk to Mr. Krumm today and see what can be done. Its a cinch he can't rent his cottage without extensive repairs, and it would pay him to open up the cave instead."

Since the tearing down of the cottage foundation wall, Miss Meadows had not been able to stay in the dwelling. She had taken a room at the hotel for one night, and after that Mr. Krumm had transferred her to another one of his cottages, directly on Morning Glory Lake.

Surprisingly, the real estate man had announced

that Miss Meadows might have the place rent free.

"You've had a rugged time of it at the other cottage," he acknowledged. "You deserve a couple of peaceful weeks."

The girls correctly surmised that Mr. Krumm's generosity was occasioned by a belated realization that Calico Cave had great commercial possibilities.

They were entirely right. In the week that followed, the real estate man bolstered up the cottage foundation again, converting the building into an office where admission tickets could be sold.

He then had carpenters construct a stairway down to the fairyland chamber, one which would serve temporarily until a more permanent installation could be made.

Sometime prior to the day on which the public was to be given its first view of the cave, Mr. Krumm visited Pine Cone Camp to present a check to Judy.

"Why, what is this?" she asked in astonishment. "Is it a contribution for the Girl Scouts?"

"You may consider it as such if you want to," he said. "It's your bonus for solving the mystery of the Calico Cottage ghost."

"That was easy because I had scientific helpers," Judy laughed. "I think Bart and Captain Hager deserve the money even more than do the Scouts."

"Don't worry about that," Mr. Krumm said a bit grimly. "They'll have a share of the profits from the cave operation. Bart saw to that. He convinced me that I couldn't manage the place without them around to look after things."

"In that case, I'll accept the check," Judy decided. "Not for myself though. I'll give it to Pine Cone Camp. Perhaps the money can be used to bring some girl to camp who otherwise couldn't afford to come."

Before departing, Mr. Krumm invited all the Scouts to a preview of the cave chamber.

"Oh, wouldn't it be fun if we could have our Court of Awards ceremony there!" Judy exclaimed. "Could we, Mr. Krumm?"

"It's all right with me," he said. "The electric lights will be in by the end of the week."

Judy spoke at once to the camp director about her plan. At first, Miss Lubell was somewhat hesitant, but after personally inspecting the cave room and the facilities which had been provided for the public, she became as enthusiastic as Judy over the prospect of holding a ceremony in the fairyland chamber.

The night set for the affair finally arrived. The Scouts enjoyed a picnic supper at the cottage grounds, after hiking to the site. Afterwards, with Bart and Captain Hager acting as guides, they descended to the underground chamber.

Electric lights, skillfully placed, gave the colorful formations ethereal effects which were quite breathtaking. The Scouts named many of the figures, giving them such titles as the Indian Oven, Woman with a Hood, the Cathedral, and Phantom Hands.

The spell of enchantment was still upon the girls as they took formation for the Court of Awards ceremony.

Miss Lubell personally presented special achievement badges to all the Scouts who had earned them. Judy, Kathleen, Ardeth, Virginia, and the other members of Beaver Patrol won honors in many fields, for dramatics, in swimming, health and for safety achievements.

Then Miss Lubell announced that for Judy and Kathleen, there was to be a special award. An expectant hush fell upon the group.

Amazed and rather embarrassed to be singled out for particular attention, the two Beaver Patrol girls stepped forward to receive the badges.

As Miss Lubell held them up, everyone burst into laughter. As a joke, the Scouts of Lone Tree had fashioned two huge medals of tin. On their face, in large letters, they had painted: "Explorer."

"Just a little memento of your exciting summer, Judy," Ardeth assured her. "You know, wherever you go, you seem to stir up fun and adventure."

"All of the Scouts do," Judy corrected. "Kathleen certainly did as much as I to earn her tin medal!"

"I just followed in your footsteps," Kathleen laughed. "Anyway, we shouldn't get the credit for producing forest fires or hi-jackers. Caves are our specialty."

"Here's hoping you find more and better ones," Ardeth chuckled, fastening the huge tin medal to Judy's Scout uniform. "Or is that possible?"

"We never could discover a more thrilling cave than Calico," Judy replied earnestly.

"But you'll try!" Ardeth teased.

Judy shook her head. Her eyes twinkled as she answered, "No, I promise you I've had enough of stalagmites and stalactites for one summer. From this hour forward, I'm spending all my idle hours at Pine Cone Camp!"